Trouble in the Air, and Under the Ground

"Sorry to say they don't much want to look at us, either," the ghost of Mark's grandfather said. "Can't say I've traveled all that much since I passed over, not that I ever thought I could until you and Mark took up together. But I can't work out what the trouble is."

He paused, and Clina's ghost jumped in sharp as a razor.

"Best tell her what you been carrying on to me about, Walt. If it's so all-fired important as you say, get it out so they might can *do* something about it."

Wisps of fear curled through Beth's belly and heart.

"I don't want to worry you, now," Mark's Papaw said. "All this is so new to me I might be mistaken, hear? But I got to tell you if feels to me like Mark is caught up in all this somehow."

Beth's own words about the two of them getting a break from all the excitement of the last few months soured and curdled in her memory.

*For everyone who works hard
to make dangerous jobs a little bit safer*

SORROWS IN THE EARTH

BOOK THREE OF THE VOICES THROUGH TIME SERIES

KARI KILGORE

SPIRAL PUBLISHING, LTD.

CHAPTER 1

MARK HERSCH KNEW he should have expected it with the elevation gain, but he was still surprised when his ears popped. He glanced at the GPS to confirm what his head already knew.

Just past four thousand feet and climbing.

The road curved through patches of shiny-leaved rhododendrons and more pines than oaks, so it made sense. Even for someone who lived in Bountyfield, Virginia, in the heart of the Appalachian Mountains, such a quick increase still required a bit of adjustment.

This stretch had the forest too close on both sides to see very far, but a couple of stunning overlooks down into the valley weren't too far ahead. Ear complaints or not, he planned to take advantage of the first time he'd been up this way for months.

Mark figured his ears could be forgiven their slow reflexes, since he'd only lived back home in Bountyfield for three months now. He still needed a bit more time to get his mountain legs under him for sure.

He'd been back about the same amount of time he'd been engaged to the amazing woman sitting next to him.

He glanced over at Beth, who as usual didn't disappoint with her humor and what he suspected was an easy ability to read his mind. She stared back at him, big blue eyes wide, and stretched her mouth open in the most adorable ear-clearing pantomime he'd ever seen.

She winked and took another sip of her ever-present coffee, reminding Mark that he still hadn't finished his. He grabbed his black travel mug and swallowed the last bits of barely sweetened brew, wishing he had more after getting up extra early for the drive.

The sunlight sparkled through Beth's brown curls where they floated just above her shoulders, and Mark hoped his own ornery strawberry blond hair wasn't too much of a mess.

She rested one hand on his shoulder as he drove, making him wish they were in her Maxima rather than his rather ponderous official blue Commonwealth of Virginia sedan. Much better snuggling possibilities in Beth's quick and nimble ride.

And she adored tearing up and down twisty mountain roads like this one more than he ever would.

"Altitude getting to you, city boy?"

"Too many years in the flatlands of Richmond," he said, winking right back at her. "I'll recover quick if they keep sending me up here to the wilds of Sutherland County."

Right on cue, a green road sign declared they were seven miles from Isom Gap. The work destination for both of them on this cool October Thursday morning, and their hiking and mini-vacation stay for the weekend.

"What time is your first meeting?"

Mark consulted his mental calendar—not quite as accurate as his internal map and orientation software, but pretty good most of the time.

"Eleven for the sit-down with the mine operators within the district. Then they'll go along on a few inspections to check out several creeks and streams, but I'm not expecting any kind of trouble. You'll be at the courthouse until what, four?"

"That I will. They're supposed to have a good supply of records and photos already pulled for me. Got a couple of local collectors meeting me today and tomorrow, with boxes full of stuff. Including my favorite glass plate negatives."

Mark smiled as he followed an especially steep and sharp curve to the right, where the trees grew so thick overhead that the morning sunlight only dappled the pavement.

He'd first met Beth not on an inspection, but during one of his talks to local landowners. Besides his work keeping an eye on coal mine runoff and doing this kind of outreach for the Department of Mines, Minerals, and Energy, he coordinated with residents as much as he could on his own pet project. Some of his co-workers called it an obsession rather than a passion, but Mark didn't care one bit about that.

They could make sure every current coal operation was keeping the waterways clear all day long, and they were doing a fine job of that. So fine that Mark loved having time to focus on finding runoff from old abandoned mines and even unpermitted house-coal pits from decades back.

The amounts might be small, but getting those small problems before they ran into creeks and rivers added up quick.

He slowed at a brown sign letting them know a scenic overlook was coming up, then pulled off the road to the left. The parking area was empty of other vehicles but scattered with drifting leaves in orange, yellow, and scarlet.

"What's this one?" Beth said, leaning forward as Mark parked close to a wooden ramp leading out to a stone tower.

3

He tried to ignore the way the only thing visible beyond was the intense blue sky dotted with pure white clouds.

"Would you believe I have no idea? I've always been in a hurry to either get up the mountain or get down. This is yet another advantage of you coming with me this weekend. I get to actually enjoy the drive."

They both stepped out into the stiff breeze that had to be a good fifteen degrees colder than Bountyfield. Mark leaned back in for his blue state jacket at the same time Beth reached for her green hoodie. She smiled as she pulled it on over his faded old Virginia Tech t-shirt.

"Hiking this weekend might be a challenge if it stays this cold."

"I'm sure we'll manage to find something to do," Mark said holding out his hand.

Beth held tight, and they headed up the ramp.

She reached for the copper necklace she almost always wore—one Mark had made for her not long after they met back in December. The charm was a fragment of one of those glass plate negatives she loved so much.

One that had shattered itself while he and Beth were engaged in a most unusual rescue. Saving a long-deceased coal miner from a rock fall in his tiny house pit before he caused more damage to everyone around him. Bringing his bones out to free his mournful ghost and let him rest at last.

The copper-lined bit of glass served as Beth's conduit to the world of ghosts. Especially to the woman in the more-than-century-old image, a sassy and extremely honest woman named Clina Jane.

As was often the case when Beth touched Mark while wearing the necklace, he heard Clina Jane's thick mountain accent himself.

"...to hauling us far off and away from home again, and for no good reason to anyone."

Beth rolled her eyes, but she was smiling. Clina Jane was at least partially responsible for getting the two of them together, and she'd done more than help rescue their lost miner before he could pull more souls down under the earth with him.

She'd been instrumental in helping understand and clear out a terrifying haunted cave right outside of Bountyfield after that, then in helping Beth rid a nearby town of a plague of moths.

Sinner moths, as it turned out.

"We both have to work over here, Clina," Beth said. "Then we'll have the first vacation we've taken together, even if it is only for a few days."

Mark heard rough laughter in the background—laughter he'd loved and known his whole life long.

"Glad you could make the trip with us, mud bug," he said.

"Wouldn't miss a chance to get out of town, water bug," his Papaw said, his voice raspy from what he called his hard-living days. "Can't remember the last time I was all the way over to Isom Gap"

Clina grunted. "Sure wish *I* didn't remember. Can't think of one single reason for it myself."

Beth squeezed Mark's hand, then let go as she stepped out onto the wooden platform around the stone tower. He knew she heard ghostly chatter like that all day long, and he was still amazed she could stand it.

Thankfully taking the necklace off gave her a bit of peace when she needed it.

And privacy when he and Beth wanted it.

"This is incredible, Mark," she said, standing with her hands on the waist-high wooden fence surrounding the circular platform.

He didn't much want to walk out that far. But he wanted

her to know he didn't especially love heights even less. If he'd known that tower's platform jutted out above a few hundred feet of sheer cliff, he might have kept driving.

After miles of the closed-in road, the vista before and beneath them truly was stunning. The valley rippled out below like frozen ocean waves streaked with autumn colors. The pine-scented wind was quite a bit stronger, too, leaving him no choice but to step close enough to grab the rail.

He focused on the ring finger of Beth's left hand to give himself a chance to catch up and catch his breath.

His grandmother's engagement ring there still looked odd to his eyes after a few weeks, but the quiet thrill of her wearing it stayed with him. The slender yellow gold band and cluster of three white diamonds had a decidedly old-fashioned look that didn't match any of her other jewelry.

Beth tried to protest when Mark insisted it was only a placeholder. A promise he was determined to keep when they finally had time to get away on a much bigger trip together. Somewhere with enough jewelry and antique shops to discover exactly the ring she wanted.

One that made her eyes light up like the day he asked her to marry him. And the much later day when he gave her the temporary ring.

Mark knew it was only a symbol, and Beth said the same herself. But he still wanted to give her a gift that brought that sweet light to her eyes every day for the rest of their lives.

"The view is impressive," he said, forcing himself to look up. "Too bad there are no signs or cell phone signal. I'm not sure what we're looking at."

"Clina informs me it wasn't near this pretty when the view meant you'd been walking or riding a dang horse all day long. Of course she says *purty* instead of pretty, but you get the idea." She stopped for a second, then scowled. "And your granddad says you're being awful brave, and he's right proud of you."

Mark raised his eyebrows and shook his head, but he didn't dare let go of the railing.

That was one of the biggest problems with ghostly relatives. They often slipped up and outed him before he was ready.

"Yeah, he's got a point," Mark said. "To tell you the truth now that he already did, I'm not a big fan of heights."

Beth blinked, then stepped closer and linked her arm through his.

"Ain't a thing to be ashamed of, Mark," his Papaw said. "Only shame is in pretending and hiding the truth."

"I had no idea," Beth said. "Sorry about that. We can go back."

He leaned down and kissed her cheek, then held his forehead against hers.

"I'll be okay, sweetheart. Look just as long as you want to. Just don't ask me to climb along the outside of the fence or shimmy down this tower."

"You got it. Much as I miss her, I guess it's just as well we didn't bring Janie. I've never tested it, but I get the feeling she wouldn't be afraid *enough* of heights."

Mark had a hard time believing Beth's sweet Redbone hound could be anything but perfect. Especially because she won his heart anew every night when she curled up against his back with a contented sigh. But he wouldn't want to be the one trying to hang onto her leash at a time like this. Or trying to keep himself calm if Beth had to.

"Okay, I guess we should go," she said. "Thank you for bringing me out here. That means a lot to me."

"You're always welcome. Don't let me stop you from seeing anything you want to, Beth. I spend more than enough time under the ground to make up for being above it once in a while."

She slipped her arm around his waist and squeezed before taking his hand again.

"Let's go see what kind of trouble we can get into in Isom Gap. We could use a break from all the excitement of the last few months."

Mark tried to convince himself his shiver was because of the chilly wind.

Not one of the weird premonitions he'd always had, a trait shared with his Papaw.

But he couldn't quite pretend it wasn't a shiver that felt like trouble.

CHAPTER 2

BETH LIKED the Sutherland County Courthouse immediately, partly because it was different.

Unlike the one in Bountyfield or many others she'd visited throughout the region, it was red brick rather than pale stone. Two floors and an impressive number of broad windows, which likely did a wonderful job of circulating air before the days of air conditioning.

The front lawn was bigger than usual as well. Rather than the building crowding right up against the sidewalk and main street, it was set back a good twenty feet. Lovely groups of bushes and flowers interspersed with a few trees helped make it look inviting rather than intimidating.

The rest of Isom Gap had the same welcoming feel, with more brick and wooden buildings, bunches of trees, and quite a few people out walking around for such a brisk day.

She hoped their tiny private cabin on the hilly outskirts of town was as nice as what she'd seen so far. Much as she missed Janie—currently being spoiled absolutely rotten by Beth's parents—the idea of a couple of days to relax and focus on Mark sounded heavenly.

She mentally promised to bring Janie along on the next trip with hiking involved so Mark could spend outdoorsy time with the sweet Redbone hound he called his number two girlfriend.

He parked behind the courthouse in a typical broad parking lot, and thank goodness her contact here had assigned several spaces close by the back door. The only other empty spots were way at the back. Carrying her scanner inside and possibly having to lug boxes full of belongings back out across yards of rippled and cracked asphalt didn't sound like a good use of her time, or Mark's muscle.

Expecting people bringing in their personal and family treasures for her Sutherland County book to make the same hike wouldn't have been the best way to gain their cooperation and trust, either.

Mark brushed back her hair, then leaned over and kissed her cheek. The light in his bright green eyes had her half glad he was looking forward to his tour with the mine operators today, and half wishing he could spend the day with her.

And she hadn't admitted it to him or anyone else, but she loved seeing him in that blue official jacket. He'd been wearing it the first time they met—along with his faded and wonderfully soft Virginia Tech t-shirt that she appropriated every chance she got—only a couple of days after she'd first heard Clina's voice.

Same with the neat reddish beard he'd regrown as the weather turned cooler.

"Course he looks handsome with a beard," Clina said in her musical mountain accent, never one to shy away from sharing her opinion. "Man ought to have a little hair on his face. Never did understand why they want to scrape and shave back to looking like little boys again."

Beth was relieved he'd gotten out of the car rather than

hearing that commentary. Even if she did agree with every word.

"To tell you the truth, Clina," Beth said under her breath as she got out herself, "I hope I can convince him to keep it year-round. Handsome as he is, he looks way too much younger than me without it."

Clina's cackle and a hearty guffaw from Mark's grandfather followed her out of the car.

Mark already had what looked like a giant black laptop bag for her scanner over his shoulder by the time she joined him, and another she'd loaded up with snacks, a thermos full of coffee, and a couple of water bottles. She hadn't yet decided if it was just his nature to carry things for her every chance he got, or if he still felt guilty about her breaking her arm back in December.

She would much prefer he did it because he wanted to. Given the chance to keep a huge ghost-flung rock from landing on his head, she'd do the very same all over again.

"Anything else you need?" he said, bumping the door closed with his hip. He did know to hand over her backpack with her laptop inside without complaining.

"This is pretty much it, assuming I don't end up taking boxes-full back home with me. A few people mentioned having books and photo albums that will be too much to scan in a couple of days."

"They're excited about you being here. Paying attention to them. I understand how they feel." He flashed the fantastic smile that had captured her full attention at first sight. "Seriously, though, you know as well as I do how many of these small towns just get ignored for decades at a time. The whole region does. Then half of what we *do* read or watch or hear about is negative or some kind of sick joke. Your books, they make people happy."

Beth had a shy and silly urge to deflect the compliment,

or at least try to tone it down in some way. But she knew from experience every word he said was true.

She'd had a few book signings over the years, and quite a few more after Bountyfield (and her articles about their adventures in the cave) made national news over the summer. The way mountain people reacted to the collection of their history, their stories told in an honest and positive way, kept her motivated.

"I just hope I can live up to those lofty expectations," she said, holding the heavy steel courthouse door open for him.

The polished tile floor of the long hallway inside reflected the morning sunlight, making it brighter than overhead bulbs could account for. A door almost at the far end stood open, and Beth heard excited voices.

A whole bunch of excited voices.

"I think that's for you, sweetheart," Mark said, touching her shoulder with his. "You're going to be busier than I am today."

She had to admit he was right before she thought up a way to deflect the intimidating idea. Beth had a feeling she was about to come face-to-face with a far more intimidating —and nerve-wracking—reality.

A silvery framed sign beside the door proclaimed this *Sutherland County Book Research Day*, with a big bold *Welcome Beth Azen!* at the bottom. Inside, more long tables than she could imagine she needed were lined up, several already covered with memorabilia.

Easily twenty people waited inside, chatting and showing off their treasures.

Every other time she'd held an event like this, not many more than that stopped by during the entire day. Even then, she'd often gotten a big enough collection from a few people to need to take work home.

From the looks of this, she could stay right here in the

courthouse for a solid week and still need to load up the car before they drove back to Bountyfield.

She glanced back at Mark, who beamed with so much pride she couldn't help grinning herself.

"Want to trade places today?"

He laughed loud enough that everyone turned their way, then leaned close enough to lower his voice.

"You're really volunteering to spend the day tromping around creeks and streams with a bunch of mine operators, who secretly appreciate what I do but enjoy arguing with me way too much to ever say so? All so I can bask in your reflected glory here with people who can't *wait* to talk to you?"

He shrugged and strolled into the room, saying "I'm game" over his shoulder.

Beth followed before he could think up too many outlandish things to tell the group.

One small woman stepped forward, not quite blending into the rest. She was around Beth and Mark's age for one thing, likely still in her thirties as opposed to almost everyone else who was decades older. She also wore a charcoal gray pantsuit that perfectly flattered her comfortable figure rather than the more colorful attire of the others.

"Mr. Azen?" she said to Mark. "So lovely to meet you! I'm Susan Mason. Let me help you get set up."

Mark turned a smartass smirk in Beth's direction. Neither of them had managed to settle on a date for their wedding, any more than she'd settled her question about whether to change her name or not.

"He's not Mr. Azen just yet," Beth said with a warm smile. "But that is one of the options we're considering. I'm Beth Azen, and this is my fiancé Mark Hersch."

Susan put both hands to her cheeks, which were turning quite red.

"Oh no, I shouldn't have just assumed. Especially since I'm married to a Harrison myself and never did make the change. I'm delighted to meet you both. Come on, we've got space all ready for you."

One of the long tables was set up along the back wall, right in front of the power outlets already supplied with a sturdy surge suppressor. On the table right next to it waited a surprisingly enticing spread of chips, cookies, candy, even individually wrapped sandwiches, alongside coffee, tea, and soda.

They'd even brought in a cooler full of ice, and another of those silvery signs that exhorted guests to *please* not eat or drink around the collection.

"The historical society took care of all of this," Susan said, "with donations from one of the grocery stores in town to help. They'll keep an eye on it today and tomorrow to make sure you don't run out. They're just so pleased to have you here. I wouldn't answer for you, Beth, but I know they'd be thrilled if you could do an interview or maybe even a talk at one of their meetings."

Beth tried to draw enough breath to answer without much success. Chatting with folks one-on-one was easy enough, and writing was easier than that. She'd hadn't felt overwhelmed by the idea of bunches of readers for her words for a long time.

But she'd never quite worked out Mark's natural ability to talk to big crowds of people no differently than he chatted over dinner with friends.

As he so often did, he understood exactly how freaked out she felt.

Even more importantly, he knew what to do about it.

He stepped forward and put both bags on Beth's table, then unzipped the one with the scanner inside. He stepped forward and shook Susan's hand.

"This all looks wonderful, Susan, thank you so much. Beth has plenty of room even if she ends up needing another scanner. Just give us a few minutes to set up before she gets started."

Susan snapped her fingers with dramatic flair.

"*That's* what I forgot. You did ask about a scanner, and we've got one pulled aside and everything. Let me send a quick text, then I'll help you get ready."

Susan whipped out her phone as she walked over to the gathered history enthusiasts. Beth let out a breath when Susan asked them to wait a bit longer.

"You okay?" Mark said close to her ear.

The knots and nerves that had been trying to colonize her body loosened at the sound of his voice.

"I'll be fine in a minute. I didn't expect this many people, and I sure didn't plan to be doing interviews or history lectures."

He rubbed her shoulder, moving down her arm until he squeezed her hand.

"Well, you don't have to talk about history, do you? I'd bet what they want to hear about is your books. Everyone else in here talks about history. Get some more coffee on board, and tell me what I can do to help before I head out."

Beth took a long sip, savoring her barely warm brew spiked with a little bit of cinnamon and ginger.

Sure, she could talk books. That's what this whole trip was about, besides the quick vacation.

"Not a thing in the world you need to worry about, Beth," Mark's Papaw said, and she heard Clina give a solid "That's *exactly* right" in the background. "These folks wanted you here for good reason. You just take a long, deep breath and have yourself a real good day."

She did exactly that, then swung her backpack around and pulled her laptop out.

"We can set up… I guess I should be in the middle, with my good scanner to my right. With all that food here, my emergency snack bag should definitely be under the table and out of sight."

"You got it, gorgeous."

By the time Susan returned, they had everything arranged and Beth's nerves were more or less behaving.

"You'll have your scanner and a loaner laptop to run it any minute now. What else can I do?"

"I think we're all set, thank you," Mark said. "I've got to get going for my own meeting that won't be nearly as interesting, so I'll leave you both to it."

Susan tilted her head and smiled, one hand on her hip.

"Oh, I don't know. That mine operator bunch can get pretty lively when they all get together. Especially when they get a cocktail or two into their bellies at dinner."

Mark's eyebrows drew down for a second.

"You're married to *Lisa* Harrison? That's fantastic! She's the only operator who cuts me a little bit of slack around here. I'll be sure to tell her how much help you've been."

Susan rolled her eyes, but she was still smiling.

"Do tell her that, please. I get the feeling she thinks I have nothing but a cushy office job and sit on my backside all day. I'll give you an introduction, Beth, so everyone will know how to behave and not scare you away. Good to meet you, Mark, and I'll give you two a minute."

Mark shook his head as she walked away.

"Out of everyone I know over here, Lisa's the one I think you'd like best. The others are good guys, but they can be a handful. All set?"

Beth eyed the people waiting—milling around with a purpose now, collecting whatever they'd brought for her.

All of them here to help her do what she loved to do anyway.

"All set. Good luck with your unruly bunch."

"You too. I'll check in around lunchtime."

A quick kiss, and he walked out, with a quick wave to the crowd.

Beth stepped behind the table, nodded at Susan, and got ready to face the adventures of the day.

CHAPTER 3

AFTER HELPING Beth set up at the courthouse, Mark was delighted all over again at how much more attention her writing got after a story of hers was picked up by national news back in July.

Their strange cave adventures certainly changed his life for the better, and continued to make things better for everyone.

The drive on to the mine inspector's field office on the other side of Isom Gap and what he hoped would be a quieter meeting only took a few minutes.

Even after the steep climb of the drive, the small down-town looked deceptively level, almost like it wasn't in the mountains at all. Only the one ridge full of coal seams at the edge of town went higher.

A bunch more of those red brick buildings lined the streets, a pleasing contrast from all the pale stone in Bounty-field. Wood houses peeked through here and there on the outside edge before the forest took over again.

The field office was tucked into one of those old wooden houses, donated and converted decades ago for county and state use by whatever agency happened to need the space.

The lack of power outlets alone confirmed how long the place had stood, and how little budget had been dedicated to its upkeep. Mark set up in what was clearly a former dining room, with a typical brown conference table jammed in with barely enough space left over for walking behind too many rolling office chairs.

He paced around anyway, rubbing the back of his neck and taking a good look at the room. He'd never bothered on several visits before, but something had him uneasy today.

Built-in cabinets and drawers made for dishes and flatware held office supplies, and tan vertical blinds took the place of handmade curtains. The energy efficient overhead light worked just fine for meetings, but Mark wondered what it had replaced. What all the original homeowners had picked out for their family and special holiday parties.

How his own grandparents might have decorated in a house that reminded him so much of theirs.

Seemed that quick few minutes of talking to his Papaw stirred up more homesickness than usual. That or his unexpected encounter with a cliff edge on the way in roughed up his nerves more than he knew.

Thankfully, mine operations in Sutherland County seemed to run smoothly in Mark's experience. Meaning safely and legally. Between that and his plan for more of a demonstration than a serious inspection, his unsettled mood shouldn't cause trouble for anyone besides himself.

From their blustery and enthusiastic greetings, the mine owners and operators expected the same thing to hold true on this visit. They arrived in a loud group, fifteen minutes early and surprised to see Mark ready and waiting.

A burly man with an aggressive gray crewcut to go with his purple golf shirt and what looked like ironed and pressed blue jeans was the first to stick out his hand. The others hung back, obviously comfortable deferring to him.

"Good to see you here so early, young man, ready to get this show on the road. Bill McConvey, McConvey Mining and Minerals right here in Isom Gap. Triple M for short, of course."

Mr. McConvey grabbed Mark's hand and squeezed too hard, pulling forward just a bit. He would have pulled Mark off balance if he hadn't been braced against the all-too-common power maneuver.

"We've met before, Mr. McConvey. Mark Hersch. Out of Richmond until a couple of months ago, when I reopened the Bountyfield office. I'm sure you know I'm not planning any kind of full inspection, but I'm ready if you have some kind of water issue underground you need me to see. Today is more about showing you more about how we monitor the waterways outside the mines."

From McConvey's satisfied smile, he remembered Mark plenty well.

Just like Mark remembered assigning a handful of minor violations to Triple M a couple of years back.

"That's right, that's right, I remember you now. Taught me a thing or two about those tiny little streams around here. Just as soon not have any more of your lessons this time around."

Mark nodded as he stepped forward to greet the other owners and operators. No matter how silly the word and personality games got, the end result of cleaner water was worth it.

"I hope everything goes well too, Mr. McConvey. We'll chat for a quick few minutes here before we head out into the field, make sure everyone knows what to expect."

Most of the men and one woman were familiar to Mark, and generally a good bunch. None of the shady big players or barely-legal wildcat operators who required constant watching to avoid major problems or an outright tragedy.

Everyone here was in it to make money, of course, like any business.

But safety mattered too.

Lisa Harrison—the one woman among them—met him with a grin. She wasn't any taller than Mark at not quite six feet, and with a strong, slender build, she wasn't especially intimidating at first sight. But he'd never seen the men give her any trouble she didn't give back, with a little extra added on for good measure.

"Heard you were over at the courthouse earlier. Got quite a crowd coming in to meet your Beth."

"They were waiting when we walked in. Susan took very good care of us."

Lisa's expression turned softer. "She does that every chance she gets. Works her ass off doing it, too. We all appreciate you two for coming up here."

Mark's thread of unease returned when they all headed out to check a handful of streams for good maintenance.

Three of the men piled into Mark's state car, including boisterous Mr. McConvey. He perched in the passenger seat and happily chattered away to the men in back.

Denny Grissom had been around almost as long as McConvey, and from what Mark heard his quiet demeanor stayed in place no matter what happened around his mines. Red hair carefully parted and combed, he nodded along to McConvey's stream of words, but he didn't share many of his own.

Chip Hackworth had only arrived from a town a few hours away a couple of years before, taking over two operations when their owners retired. He guffawed loud enough to make Mark wince, and kept raising his voice to try to get his own jokes and tales into the car's already crowded air. His brown hair got more and more stirred up as he brushed it back every time he wanted to talk.

None of that explained Mark's growing sense that he was missing something. More than a bunch of "That ain't nothing, listen to this…" jawboning could explain, even at high volume.

He pretty much always wished Beth was with him, and her after-hours commentary on this crowd would no doubt have him laughing until his ribs ached. He suspected they never would have seen her razor-sharp wit coming once she got comfortable. Not before they were right up against it.

Right now, he wished for the insight and downright spying Clina and his Papaw could sometimes offer in situations like this.

And he wondered if his own ghostly interaction-by-association was somehow sharpening his own senses.

So he really should have been better prepared when his phone buzzed in his pocket, rather than jumpy enough to nearly drop his whole sample kit into a merrily bubbling creek. He might have gotten away with that, but his grunt and curse was too much to ignore.

Especially since he followed in his Granny's proud tradition of making that curse a hearty "Shit fire." Twisted and smoothed into her proper "*Shit*fahr!" to make it locally appropriate.

Of course that gave Bill McConvey and Chip Hackworth the opportunity to roar laughter while they pounded each other on the back. The others gathered around to watch the demonstration of how the sampling worked laughed under their breath, shaking their heads, probably at the leader's antics.

"Tadpole jump up and get you?" McConvey said, wiping his eyes.

"Guess that means this creek can't be *too* polluted, huh?"

Hackworth chimed in. "Or else it's got so bad the tadpoles mutated and grew teeth."

Mark smiled and shrugged. Giving himself time to think of something clever or silly to say, he held the tiny test tube in the clear, freezing-cold water, pushed a black rubber cork into the top, and pulled off his blue gloves. He'd labeled all of the tubes the day before in his precise handwriting, so all he had to do was drop it beside several others inside what looked like a miniature blue lunchbox.

"We'll leave that up to the Commonwealth to judge," he said, getting to his feet. "But if you happen to spot some of those toothy tadpoles, do me a favor and round a few of them up for me."

That set all of them off in a calmer, far more friendly round of laughter. Even quiet Denny Grissom nodded and smiled.

Mark took the chance to step to the side and check his phone before they headed out and away from the rare bit of cellular signal. He wasn't sure between his kneeling position and running explanation of what he was doing, but that felt like the buzzing pattern for a message from Beth.

Sure enough...

So sorry to bother you, Sweetie, I know you're busy. Getting some seriously odd chatter on the inside this afternoon. More than usual. Might be something strange going on here, and it might involve you. Maybe someone you're with? Either way, talk soon. Love you.

He checked the time, relieved to see it was close enough to one o'clock to call it a day, or at least break for lunch.

"I think that has us wrapped up for now," he said, rejoining the group. "I'd be glad to answer any questions or show you more about what we do, but I have to admit I'm starting to get hungry. Anyone care to join me for lunch?"

As Mark hoped and half-expected, Bill McConvey waved his hand toward Mark's car.

"Seeing as how I'm riding with you, that only makes sense." He turned to the others. "Rest of y'all come on, meet up at the Brew Crew."

Much as he'd prefer to have Beth all to himself before he had to go back to the field office and bury his head in paperwork, Mark wasn't about to miss the chance to hear what she had to say.

And maybe more importantly, what had her lively ghosts so stirred up.

"Any chance this bunch can manage to behave yourselves if my fiancé joins us?"

Before any of the men could ramp up with leers and lewd comments, Lisa elbowed her way to the front. Just as Mark expected, she proved she more than held her own by the way the men let her pass.

Even more so when they let her talk without interference.

"They'll manage to behave," she said, glaring at each of her fellow operators in turn. "Or as my own grandmother used to say, they'll soon have reason to wish they had. I'd sure like to meet your fiancé, Mr. Hersch."

Mark nodded and smiled his thanks, then sent a quick note to Beth, asking her to walk over to the Brew Crew. He'd already planned to take her to dinner there sometime over the weekend, for good food and excellent beer and cider.

At the very least, Beth's curious and investigative nature would be sure to get a kick out of this crowd. Hopefully she was having as much fun with hers.

CHAPTER 4

Susan Mason was true to her word, giving Beth a great introduction and establishing ground rules at the same time. Even with the already big group and more people coming in all the time, no one crowded around Beth at her table.

She wasn't sure if Susan passed the word to the new arrivals or if someone else did.

Either way, Beth appreciated it greatly.

An orderly line stayed consistent, bringing a bigger variety of photos, postcards, and newspaper articles than she expected. But the real surprise was the fascinating array of other treasures they carried.

Medals and prizes, ranging from local schools or civic groups to larger organizations, all the way to recognition for military service going as far back as the Spanish-American and Civil Wars. A surprising number were for their ancestors' military service in other countries—reflecting nearly the same diverse collection of settlers Beth found in Bountyfield.

People brought birth, marriage, and death certificates from long decades ago. Trinkets from vacations taken long before they were born. A fascinating array of political buttons and memorabilia.

Even with Susan making sure everyone signed the release forms and Beth scanning quite a few of the items while they waited, people were still visibly nervous as they handed things over. As if they expected her to grind them under her heel, or maybe clutch their treasures to her chest and dart out of the room, never to return.

People seemed oddly segregated, too. Remaining in separate groups and chatting, even while waiting in line. Beth was certain several of them turned their bodies to hide whatever they were showing her from anyone else on the other side of the divide.

She finally took a break after a couple of hours, heading down the hall to walk around and shed some of the coffee she'd been sipping all morning. The truth was she wanted a chance to talk to Clina and Mark's Papaw every bit as much as a break from talking to everyone else.

"Do either one of you see anything strange going on here? People are very friendly to me, and to some of the others. But I swear bunches of them seem to think their neighbors have knives hidden under their shirts."

"Don't know for sure why," Clina said, "but you got it pegged right. Folks don't even cross paths to *look* for knives on this side. Just stay bunched up in their own corners glaring at each other."

Beth stood beside the window at the front of the courthouse, looking over the red brick buildings and black and brown roofs of Isom Gap. People bustled around in the bright sunshine, visiting the restaurants and shops that always clustered around the county seat.

She couldn't tell from there if two separate groups were avoiding each other as carefully as she'd seen all morning.

"They're actually on opposite sides?" she said. "Truly staying apart?"

"Sure are," Mark's Papaw said. "Not even taking a glance toward the others. Like if they turn and look, they'll turn into pillars of salt same as Lot's wife in that Bible story."

"Will any of them talk to you?"

"Sorry to say they don't much want to look at us, either," he said. "Can't say I've traveled all that much since I passed over, not that I ever thought I could until you and Mark took up together. But I can't work out what the trouble is."

He paused, and Clina jumped in sharp as a razor.

"Best tell her what you been carrying on to me about, Walt. If it's so all-fired important as you say, get it out so they might can *do* something about it."

Wisps of fear curled through Beth's belly and heart.

"I don't want to worry you, now," Mark's Papaw said. "All this is so new to me I might be mistaken, hear? But I got to tell you if feels to me like Mark is caught up in all this somehow."

"All this?" Beth said. "You mean the town itself? Or the way people won't look at each other? I don't understand."

"Yeah, I was afraid of that. It's more like…some of the trouble is pointing toward him. Or maybe he can serve some kind of a purpose. I sure am sorry, Beth. I can't work it out any better."

Beth covered her mouth with one hand, shaking her head.

Her own words about the two of them getting a break from all the excitement of the last few months soured and curdled in her memory.

"It's okay, Papaw. We're all new to this, really. It hasn't even been a year since I first heard Clina. I'll let Mark know, and we'll see what we can do about it."

She'd just finished sending a text message to him, fully

aware it might take a while before he got cell signal, when Susan popped her head out the door. When she caught sight of Beth, she crossed the distance in a few quick steps and looked out the window herself.

"Have I made them wait too long?" Beth said.

"No, not at all. Don't you worry one bit. I just stepped out to see if *you* needed anything. People are just thrilled with you and how it's all going. I hope you're finding things you can use for your book."

"Oh yeah, more than I expected. You think there will be more people tomorrow?"

"I expect you'd get another room full if you want to. I can help if you want, now that everyone seems to know the routine. Maybe run that laptop and second scanner on the easy things?"

Beth sighed and leaned against the warm window.

"That would be fantastic. The biggest holdup is waiting on my scanner and the software to do their work. I hate to make people wait when they're already so…"

Susan's brow wrinkled for a second.

"Is something wrong?"

"No, not really." Beth shook her head, wishing she'd thought before that slipped out. "It just seems like there's some kind of tension or something in the air. Everyone's been as friendly as can be to me, that's not a problem at all. I'm probably imagining the rest."

"You're not imagining a thing," Susan said with a sad smile. "You're catching the echoes of a very old, very upsetting problem Isom Gap has been dealing with since before the turn of the twentieth century. Not quite as violent as the famous feud over in Kentucky, thank goodness. But it's ongoing for sure."

"I had no idea," Beth said, even though it matched exactly what Clina and Mark's Papaw said, along with the way she'd been feeling all day. "I don't want to seem nosy or rude, but is there anything I should be careful talking about? Or writing about?"

Susan pursed her lips, staring down at her own hands.

"I hadn't really thought about it, but you do need to know if you're going to write about our little town. None of this is in the tourist brochures, of course. I can't deny it's part of our history."

She looked into Beth's eyes.

"From what I can understand from all the conflicting stories, there was an awful incident way back in the logging days. The only thing I've been able to verify is one young man was killed and another badly injured. People argue about that part, too. The real problem is no one can agree all these years later about what happened. Was it on purpose, more like a murder? Or was it truly an accident, and no one caused it at all? I'm afraid what you're picking up on is over a hundred years of mistrust."

Beth thought back to the dozens killed in mining accidents in Bountyfield, and easily that many again in other ways. So many of them going back to the lost and lonesome miner she and Mark had finally rescued.

In a strange way, the idea of focusing so much attention on one death here felt much more sensible than decades of accepting so many losses as normal in her own hometown.

"That's awful," she said. "I'm guessing there are no written records that could clear it all up."

"Not that anyone has ever found. Only a note of the results in the newspaper at the time. After all these years, I'm not sure if proof would help all that much. I swear, it's like people who aren't even related to the original families are *born* with strong opinions on one side or the other."

Beth let out a long, slow breath.

"I'll have to be very careful if I decide to write about that, you're right. I appreciate the warning."

"I hope I haven't scared you away from the project altogether. We really do have fascinating history, even if you leave that aside."

Beth couldn't help smiling at the worry in Susan's voice, as if she were a little kid asking a teacher if she could read her favorite book at the end of class. No wonder, with a dispute deep and enduring enough to divide the living and the dead.

"Not even a little bit," she said, turning back toward the room still full of people. "You mentioned reading my story of what went on in Bountyfield over the summer. All I'll say is things got a good bit stranger than what I was willing to let out to the press."

Susan raised her eyebrows and grinned.

"I had a good idea you wouldn't scare easy. Fair warning, though. If I can't talk you into spilling all the bizarre details about Bountyfield sometime, Lisa will make it her life's mission to find out."

At all the grateful and welcoming smiles when they walked back in—even if they were from two separate groups —Beth knew she was going to put *some* kind of book together for Isom Gap.

Whether it told the tale of the tragedy here remained to be seen.

She had a sneaking suspicion she'd get a lot more information to work with before she and Mark headed back home.

CHAPTER 5

THE BREW CREW pub was a sleek establishment of all concrete and steel that could have been in downtown Richmond as easily as remote Isom Gap. A row of huge, gleaming silvery tanks lined one wall, and a bunch of equally large televisions took up the other.

All the lighting fixtures looked more like metal sculptures worked and shaped perfectly around naked bulbs than anything available for sale at the hardware store.

The pleasant aroma of beer mixed with hamburgers and fries set Mark's appetite into demanding motion, reminding him that breakfast in Bountyfield was a long time ago.

His ears were grateful everything was turned down low enough to allow for conversation rather than more gleeful shouting.

By the time he walked in with his passengers, the other operators had already pulled two of the polished black metal tables together in the fairly empty restaurant section. Apparently the lunch crowd in Isom Gap ate early and moved on.

They made a show of leaving an empty seat beside Mark without too much ribbing, with Lisa Harrison on the other side. Beth strolled in and took her place before the waiters had a chance to bring menus and water.

"I understand you're dining with a bunch of shy, retiring types?" she said, glancing around the table. "Don't worry, everyone. Beth Azen. I'm here to keep the big, bad inspector reined in so you can all enjoy your lunch in peace."

A few rather undignified snorts made it out, but more of that companionable laughter showed how well she'd introduced herself. Lisa in particular seemed impressed.

Mark met Beth's gaze with a slow smile, thrilled all over again to have her beside him.

When everyone quieted down to have a look at the menus, she put her hand on his leg under the table. It was enough to bring Clina through loud and clear.

"...to tell that man of yours something is *wrong* here. Got him where he can hear me?"

"He's right here, Clina," Beth murmured. She spoke out loud to Lisa. "How's their cheeseburger?"

"Listen right close to me, then," Clina said, her voice snappish. "I ain't been up here in these parts since I was a girl myself, barely old enough to know what marrying meant. Did it anyway, and that took me away for good. Least I thought it did. Beth dragging us back here proves it over everything that I was right to go."

"Something flat out don't make sense here, Mark," his Papaw said. "There's plenty of other folks like us. The ones that crossed over into this side of life. But they're...bunched up somehow. Got themselves backed up into sides that never do mix or mingle."

Cheeseburger question answered, Beth leaned a bit closer.

"There's a long-standing feud here," she said quietly. "Goes back over a hundred years, and everyone on both sides is split over it. The tension on their side got worse over the last couple of hours. Clina, is there an actual *wall* through the middle of town on your side, or something like it?"

Mark shared Beth's wish that they could actually see into Clina's world rather than just hearing about it. But they'd never been able to work out a way to make that happen.

Luckily Clina was damn good with words and more than happy to share them.

"Call it a wall if you want to, don't make much difference from where I'm standing. They're split up into groups that won't talk to each other, nor talk much to me or your Papaw either. But that don't change the fact that something is *wrong* here. Bad. Spoiled, maybe."

Chills raced over Mark's flesh at her words, so similar to what he'd been thinking that morning. He hesitated long enough to echo Beth's choice of a cheeseburger and fries, opting for a Coke rather than anything alcoholic. Most folks around the table added either beer or cider to their orders.

He turned his head toward Beth, doing his best to pitch his words for her ears, and her ghosts.

"Something in town, you mean? Or something with the ground or water?"

What Beth called the radio in her head was quiet for a moment except for the sounds of Clina and Mark's Papaw talking softly to each other.

"Can't tell for sure which way that goes," Papaw said. "But what we both get clear as day is you're right in the middle of it, water bug."

Beth squeezed his leg before she let go to take a long drink of her own Coke.

"So, planning to take me on a tour of some of these test sites when you're finished this afternoon?" she said in her normal voice. "That could be great background for the Sutherland County book I'm putting together."

"I'd be glad to. Unless these folks have good reasons why we shouldn't."

Everyone nodded and agreed in the midst of sampling their own beverages.

Bill McConvey spoke up in nowhere near his normal booming voice.

"Get a good turnout for your project, Miss Azen? My wife and her sister were awful excited to hear what you're planning. That story you wrote about that crazy cave over in Bountyfield was a mighty fine piece of storytelling."

Mark sat back, not sure whether the man was trying to be kind or insulting. The admiration in his eyes and nods all around the table tilted the balance toward kind.

"A great turnout," Beth said. "I believe I met your wife and your sister first thing. They had a bunch of fantastic photos. Your collection of coal scrip from all around the county is going to make a great feature for the book if you'll allow me to use it. And please, call me Beth."

Mark watched blustery Bill blush all the way up to his aggressive hair, amazed as usual at how expertly Beth put people at ease. They never seemed to realize how neatly she brought them over to her side without seeming to make any effort at all.

She was uncomfortable in front of big crowds, sure. But once she settled in, Beth handled people every bit as well as he did himself. Maybe even better.

She gripped his leg again, hard, and he let her take over the conversation. It had turned entirely to what everyone else might be able to bring her for the book, anyway. Probably exactly the way she meant it to. He held one hand up to rub his nose since he'd never quite figured out how to communicate with the other side without using his mouth.

"Are you feeling something dangerous, Papaw? Do we need to get out of here tonight instead of staying over?"

"Not dangerous that way, no. More like something that might *turn* bad. What Beth said about a wall feels more right than I can figure out how to say. It's not just how no one will much talk to us. They just huddle up and stare. I feel like they're hiding things on both sides, more than some old quarrel. Things that could cause trouble here and on your side."

"Same thing as I'm getting," Clina said, frustration clear in her voice. "When me and Beth went over to Estonoa to visit, folks were awful happy to see a new face. Like to talk my ear off with all the tales they just *had* to tell. Here? Even though I was born here myself and know some of the ones that's passed? Feels more like a right mess of mean and angry. Keeping something hid that shouldn't be."

"Okay," Beth said, this time as she leaned out of the way for the waiter to put down her burger and fries. "Are you feeling like this bad thing is here, in town? Or out where Mark was earlier today?"

"Out with him, I'd wager," Papaw said. "I feel it some right now, like smoke from a fire you put out, but that smell lingers in the air. Not near as strong as it was before."

Mark took his turn to lean in, even though his mouth and stomach were rather rudely demanding he pay attention to his own food. The golden-brown fries were still steaming, and the cheese was visibly soft from the heat of the burger.

"Then we'll head out there as soon as we both finish work for the evening. We might pick up more along the way, especially with Beth at the courthouse. Hopefully getting out in the field while we're all together will let you see what's wrong. I have to tell you, I didn't understand what was happening, but I felt...uneasy this morning, then again right before you sent me that text. I sure would like to find out why."

He looked up just in time to see Chip Hackworth hold

up his glass full of frothy beer, and Bill McConvey and the others joining him.

"To Mark and Beth," Chip said, grinning. "And the start of a long, happy life together. Maybe he'll go a little easier on us once he's an old married man, huh?"

"I wouldn't count on it," Beth said. "My Redbone hound is teaching him all her tricks for sniffing out trouble."

Mark took the golden opportunity to give her a quick peck on the cheek since the operators were already hooting and hollering. Even Lisa Harrison joined in, and Denny Grissom shook his head and smiled.

"Just one of the many ways you make my life better, sweetheart."

CHAPTER 6

THE GREAT FOOD and surprisingly good company kept Beth going through the afternoon.

Her increasing anxiety over what could possibly be targeting Mark kept her more and more on edge.

Growing noises of ghostly fussing and quarrelling inside her head had her tempted to take off her necklace several times. But she didn't want to lose the connection in case Clina and Mark's Papaw managed to find out something they could use.

Assuming the local spirits ever decided to talk to them, of course. That seemed less likely with every minute that passed.

Her temporary office at the courthouse was even more busy, so at least the time passed quickly. The curiously divided groups got into a weird pattern of taking turns stepping up to talk to her.

No one said a word about it. They just shifted back and forth into the line, almost like the closing teeth of a zipper.

Aside from her worry about Mark and the rising scent of warm electronics from not one but two scanners going, the afternoon turned out to be more pleasant the she expected.

About half an hour before she planned to lock everything up for the day, a shy woman who'd been hovering around the edges finally worked her way to Beth's table. It was the first time all day long that no one else was in line, though plenty of folks lingered to chat and discuss the treasures other people left.

The woman had red hair caught back in a smooth ponytail, and wore a simple black dress that fell well below her knees. She clutched the strap of a plain white messenger bag slung across the front of her body with both hands.

After glancing furtively at everyone else—including Susan busily scanning fragile letters a few feet away—she finally stepped up in front of Beth. She put her signed release form down with shaking hands.

Beth added it to the stack beside her and smiled.

The woman's bright smile in return was more of a surprise than Beth wanted to admit.

"Miss Azen, ma'am? I'm real sorry to bother you when I can see how busy you've been all day long. It's real good, all this hard work you're doing for our little town and county. Seems like everyone else forgot we exist up here."

Beth smiled, trying not to look as puzzled as she felt.

"I'm Beth, and you're quite welcome. I'm happy to put a book together, especially with so many people coming by to help today. I'll have a bigger job deciding what to leave out instead of looking for things to put in."

She waited, still smiling up at the woman, eyebrows raised.

"Oh, I'm so sorry. My name is Deborah Fleming, guess I should have told you that right up front. I've lived here in Isom Gap all my life. My family goes all the way back to the founding, back before this place even had a name."

"Pleased to meet you, Miss Fleming. Did you have something for me? For the book, I mean?"

Beth did her best not to jump when Clina whispered.

"Best be careful, Beth. Something ain't quite right with this one."

"I'm not sure if this kind of thing would be good for your book or not," Miss Fleming said, leaning closer. "That all depends on who's doing the reading. I got the feeling you might want to see it, at least, and make up your own mind."

She flipped open the messenger bag, and Beth was certain she wanted to take another glance around to make sure no one was sneaking up behind her, but she managed not to. She pulled out an ordinary tan folder and slid it across the table.

Beth forced herself not to imagine all the shocking or gory or embarrassing things that could possibly be inside before she opened the folder. She'd seen and heard a few things over the years that never made it into any book. Images and stories she very much wished she could forget.

The picture looked a lot like the dozens of others she'd looked at, scanned, and made notes about all day long. An old black and white, with the edges slightly curled and the tiny cracks and wrinkles of age all across the surface. About the same size as the folder Miss Fleming carried it in.

A group of men posed—one row kneeling and the other standing behind—in front of massive, towering piles of lumber that Beth would have been afraid to walk through. She couldn't imagine how they'd gotten them stacked so high, or why they wanted to.

On a closer look, she realized quite a few of the men were barely boys with smooth faces and downright scrawny bodies.

Tiny print at the bottom declared the men "Fleming Lumber Record Breaking Crew!"

"This is wonderful, Miss Fleming. Is this from your family collection?"

She frowned and shrugged with one shoulder, but her shining eyes gave away how pleased she really was at Beth's words.

"I don't know that you could call it a collection. I don't have much besides what you have in front of you. But that's the one that really matters." She leaned in again, close enough that Beth smelled perfume exactly like fresh lilacs. "That there is the very crew that was at work the day that poor boy got killed, what started all the trouble around here. This picture is from only a couple of days before he died."

This time Beth fought the urge to immediately turn to Susan for confirmation. Miss Fleming hadn't tried to hide the way she made sure no one was looking, taking care that no one besides Beth could see the photo.

Betraying that trust now—strange as it may seem—was no way to get to use the image or help solve any sort of long-running feud.

"Do you know who the crew members were?" Beth said. "I can go ahead and scan it to make the image a lot bigger if that would help."

Miss Fleming flashed her warm smile again and tapped the picture with one short fingernail.

"All you have to do is flip it over. Got the list of all the names anyone living is likely to remember right there on the back."

Beth closed the folder and turned it over instead, not wanting to accidentally put yet another wrinkle on the fragile paper.

She kept her thoughts about her own ways to figure out the names of the dead to herself.

Sure enough, two rows of neat handwriting stretched across the creased and stained backing paper. A series of local-sounding names, a few with question marks for first or last, and a couple with only question marks.

One name was circled in black ink, with a thin line drawn through the middle.

Jacob Stanley.

Beth turned the image over and counted the faces in the front row until she came to one who was most definitely a boy. It was hard to tell with the faded black and white, but his hair was fine and pale, his face and body past slender and into too thin.

But he knelt with a proud smile, staring right into the camera.

"I only heard a little bit about this earlier today," Beth said. "I know it caused trouble that hasn't let up ever since. This Jacob Stanley is the one who was killed?"

As Beth expected, Susan froze, pretending to stare at her laptop's screen. No doubt taking in every word.

"That's the one," Miss Fleming said, her cheeks flushing. "Now one of my kin was working that day, and I've always heard he swore the whole thing was *caused* by Jacob Stanley. Maybe not trying to make trouble, you understand, but getting in too much of a rush with his work. The other one who gets blamed, he tried to catch that boy's attention and got hurt for his trouble."

"Do you know which one that was?" Beth said. "The other one who got hurt?"

Miss Fleming nodded once and tapped one of the men standing in the back. This one was clearly an adult, with broad shoulders and a full beard as dark as his hair. He wasn't looking at the unseen photographer, but off to the side.

Beth started to turn the photo over again.

"I can tell you his name if that's what you're after. It's Purvis Lee Hackworth."

Susan coughed just then, and jumped up.

"I am so sorry, Beth, got something down the wrong pipe. I'll be right back."

She hurried out into the hall, doing a convincing job of clearing her throat the whole way. After hearing the same last name as one of her wife's fellow coal operators, Beth understood exactly why.

In such a small town, especially an isolated one like this, names didn't change all that often with time passing. She herself had eaten lunch with Chip Hackworth.

Unfortunately, Miss Fleming's pinched and upset face made it clear she'd probably made some of the same connections.

"You say he tried to help Mr. Stanley?" Beth said. "This Purvis Hackworth?"

"That's how I always heard it told. A whole lot of other men and boys were there that day, as you can see. I'm sure their own families have their own way of saying it. Might be other copies of this same picture for all I know."

Beth nodded, flashing her best *wow, this is an amazing find!* smile.

"Well, they may have copies, but no one has brought one in for me to see today. These names on the back make it into a real treasure. I'd love to scan it for the historical value, and maybe even for the book. All with your permission, of course."

Miss Fleming blinked, then stared down at her hands for a few seconds. She spoke in a soft voice without looking up.

"I always heard no one would want to see any of this old junk, especially about such a bad thing in our town. I'd be honored if you want to scan it, ma'am."

Beth raised the lid on her scanner, shaking her head.

"The honor is mine, truly. We might even be able to get some help filling in those blanks for the other names. But all of this is only if you call me Beth. Okay?"

Flushing bright red, Miss Fleming held out her hand for Beth to shake.

"That sounds like a good deal to me, Beth. You can call me Deborah. Mind if I watch what you do?"

Beth saw Susan walking slowly back into the room, coughing fit apparently under control, taking the time to speak to everyone she passed. Beth picked the photo up by the edges and placed it face down on the scanner's glass surface.

"Sure, of course you can watch. It only takes a couple of minutes to get the basic scan. I do any touchup that's needed later on."

She closed the lid and turned her laptop halfway around as she tapped the command to scan. The low electronic whine let her know everything was working, and a light bright enough to escape around the edges of the lid creeped along from one end of the scanner.

"It's capturing the image now," Beth said. "I'll turn it over to get the back, and I'll be finished. How do you want to be credited in the book if I end up using it?"

"Oh no, I wouldn't want that, thank you," Deborah said, holding up both hands. "I marked that down on my permission form and everything. Some folks in my family weren't real pleased when my auntie left all the old photos and things to me, not one little bit. That would just stir up all kinds of trouble for me again."

"That's perfectly fine. We have several anonymous donations every time I do one of these books. I just credit those as 'From a generous supporter.' How about that?"

Beth pointed at her laptop screen, where a clear image of the photo popped up right on cue. Deborah's eyes lit up again.

"A generous supporter sounds just fine, yes. If you can work it that way, I have a whole bunch more from the old lumber company. Photos, awards, old letters. All that stuff you can take with you if you want. This one I wanted to be careful of, you understand."

Beth opened the scanner's lid, gently turned the photo over, and hit scan again. She could just about feel how hard Susan was listening, even as she worked on scanning more printed correspondence.

"That would be fantastic," she said. "I've got several boxes ready to take back to Bountyfield with me already. People brought in a lot more than I expected, so I'd be working all through the night and on 'til Monday trying to scan if folks didn't trust me to work at home."

She slipped the photo back into its folder, slid it back across the table, and smiled up at Deborah as she turned her laptop back around for typing.

"There you go. I'll be here the same hours tomorrow too, if you want to bring your other things by. That release form you already signed will cover everything. I'll just let you add notes to it for whatever you decide to bring. Is there anything else you want to tell me about this picture?"

Deborah put the folder back into her messenger bag, chewing her lip the whole time. When she looked up, her eyes were red around the edges.

"I never have known what to think about all of this. The trouble over that poor Stanley boy, and people picking sides over it for all these long years. Trying to drag my family into it because some of them owned that sawmill way back then. I do know some folks will never believe a word of what you write in your book. I hope that doesn't cause you any trouble like I've had, Beth."

She nodded once, bobbing her body down into almost a curtsey, then turned and walked out.

Beth counted to ten, then looked toward Susan, who grinned right back at her.

"Are you kidding me?" Susan said, jumping up to stand

beside Beth. "Someone just brings that photo in after over a hundred *years*?"

"Right here in front of me. Do you know anything about her? Deborah Fleming?"

Susan bent low to get a close look at the image of the workers.

"Not much besides her doing regular courthouse business. She's absolutely right about people giving the Flemings trouble about this mess. As if any of them living now were involved, or could do a damn thing about it."

Beth shrugged and switched the view to the back of the picture and all those names.

"I don't know, Susan. Deborah might have done something about it just now. How about I send you both images so you can get a closer look? Someone in this town has to know the missing names."

"That reminds me, or at least seems like a good time to mention this. I can see very well how swamped you are with pictures and such already. But I've got a room at home just jammed full of old historical stuff my Dad rescued from a hoarder in town. The historical society wasn't interested when he talked to them for some silly reason. I didn't want to take up all your time here, but I'd love to show you sometime."

"A big collection like that can have a lot of things that were valuable to someone, but you never can figure out why. But there's always a bunch of treasure for anyone willing to look. I'd love to see it."

Susan grinned again and almost floated back to her laptop.

"What do you think over on that side?" Beth whispered. "Find anyone willing to talk about Fleming Lumber? Or Jacob Stanley and Purvis Lee Hackworth?"

"No one will give us the time of day just yet," Mark's

Papaw said. "Wonder if they'd be willing to talk if we mention those names?"

"Might be willing to run us out of town a lot faster," Clina said. "Can't say I remember any of that happening or anything about it. I might have been long gone and headed for Bountyfield by then. If we hear so much as a whisper, we'll pass it right along to you, Beth."

CHAPTER 7

THEIR DEPARTURE TIME of four got stretched out to nearly five by the time Beth finished scanning the best of the treasured items people were reluctant to leave overnight. Mark didn't mind one bit to wait.

He was fascinated by the collection, and by the side of her work he'd only rarely seen besides in the form of one of the beautiful finished books. And even more fascinated by watching her interact with people. He didn't think he could possibly be more proud of her, but seeing how thrilled people were by her attention had him full to bursting.

Beth even put him to work running the courthouse's scanner on easy things like the correspondence without tricky colorful letterhead once Susan Mason went home for the day. Mark wasn't about to attempt anything that required her expert eye. But he felt more or less competent to put paper on the glass, line it up straight against the edge, close the lid, and hit scan.

By the time everyone else left—happy and excited at lending their treasures to the project—stacks and boxes still covered almost all of the tables. Including a heavy wooden box full of Bill McConvey's coal scrip, carefully organized and tucked into tiny white envelopes the same size as the coins themselves.

Beth shut down her equipment, stood, and stretched, leaning back with her arms over her head. Mark's naughty little boy side leapt to the front of his mind at the peek of her stomach under his old t-shirt.

Not that that part of him was ever far away when he was with her.

"Ready to focus on something else?" she said, walking over and wrapping her arms around his waist.

Mark leaned over and kissed her neck, breathing in the intoxicating scent of her skin right below where she'd pushed her hair behind her ear.

"So many ways I could answer that," he whispered. "But I suppose we have other priorities tonight."

His Papaw's chuckle warned him right before Clina spoke up.

"Hope you two can spare a couple minutes to figure out this trouble they got here. Course that's only if you can see your way clear with all the other stuff you got keepin' you busy."

"And there you have it," Beth said, her lips against Mark's ear tingling all the way down his body. "I promise we'll have time for other activities. Without all the company."

"I'll look forward to that. What were you thinking? Back out where I was today?"

Beth nodded, gathering up everything that would go into her backpack before the laptop got tucked inside last. The only time she'd ever let Mark carry that was when she was recovering from a broken arm after their encounter with the lost coal miner. He would gratefully accept any help the courthouse was willing to provide to load the rest up tomorrow afternoon.

"Sure, I'd love to see the site," she said. "But I have to tell you what happened this afternoon. Have you heard talk about the feud here, going back to the old logging days?"

"Nothing specific. Just rumors of some kind of bad blood. Some folks don't like to deal with others, that kind of thing. To be honest, I never paid that much attention."

"I promise you some of the men you were with today know about it. Especially the overly enthusiastic Mr. Hackworth."

When she finished, Mark was glad she hadn't put the laptop away just yet. He would have hated to ask her to get it back out, but he would have done it. He drew breath to ask to see Purvis Lee Hackworth, but she zoomed right to it before he could say a word.

"I'm no expert at this kind of thing," he said, "but he could be related to our motormouth. Seems to have the same kind of shape to his face. You'll also notice he's looking off to the side, maybe getting ready to find someone else to talk to. Anyone on the other side have any ideas?"

"They both stayed uneasy all day," Beth said, tucking her laptop into the backpack. "Even after lunch. No one will talk to them yet. They said it got less tense when you met me for lunch. Clina said it feels like a lot more people on her side were gathered wherever you were when I sent you that text. That was one of your test sites, right?"

"The last place we stopped. I picked it because it's right on the boundary between more than one operation. Well no, that's not quite right. What I should say is creeks from three different sites drain into the stream right there."

He pulled the door closed, twisting the handle to make sure it locked. The hallway was dark except for sunlight streaming through a big window with old rippled glass at the end. The courthouse folks were glad to do what they could to help Beth, even if it meant letting her stay a little after-hours.

"Huh," Beth said as they walked slowly along the speckled white tile floor. "So you'd have to go upstream to figure out where bad water was coming from. Kind of like we had to at the cave in Bountyfield."

Mark shuddered, remembering the horrible stench of Scatterland Creek. And the dreadful things they'd found along the bottom and inside its headwaters cave.

"Hopefully not anywhere near that bad. Not that steep up here, either. But yeah, if I needed to figure out which mine was causing the trouble, I'd be hiking upstream."

He held the heavy steel door open as they stepped out into the late afternoon. The sun was at the tree line rather than behind a mountain like it would have been in Bounty-field, another sign of the higher elevation. But the air was much cooler, and the sky already faded from blue to nearly purple.

"In other words," Beth said, "with the way our luck goes, it's a good thing we're already dressed for a hike."

Mark laughed as they got into his car, but he couldn't find a thing to argue with in what she said.

"And a good thing you charmed everyone at lunch. All three of the owners gave us permission to go up there this evening. I still want you to teach me how you do that."

"I keep telling you it's a natural talent. You just have to keep watching and learning."

"I think I'd be better off letting you handle the charm-ing," Mark said, "so folks pay less attention to me. Speaking of attention, I want to hear more about what all you found today for your book, and all the unusual people you met to go with Deborah Fleming."

The drive back out along narrow roads lined with trees was pure bliss compared to the first trip that morning. Mark infinitely preferred Beth's low, sexy voice to Bill McConvey and Chip Hackworth cackling and winding each other up.

Especially when she talked about her work.

The quick turns of her mind and her obvious passion and excitement reminded him every day of how much his life had changed for the better since she became part of it.

He turned off along a graveled road for the last bit, one that curved out of sight of the main road within seconds. A maintenance road for the mining operations better suited for trucks and heavy equipment than his sedan, but more than passable.

Beth touched his arm as he parked at the wide area with good access to the stream they needed, then slipped down to holding his hand. Clina sounded as close to afraid as he'd ever heard her.

"We was right about the trouble being near you, Mark. The way we told you folks split themselves up back in town? It's a whole bunch worse out here."

A low, restless noise sounded under her voice, and Mark stared wide-eyed at Beth when he realized what he was hearing.

"How many people are here, Clina?" he said. "On your side, I mean. That sounds like a huge crowd."

"More than I ever seen when I lived here, or anywhere else for that matter. Pushed up together on one side and the other, with a great space in between."

"Are you two safe?" Beth said. "You and Papaw?"

"I reckon we're all right," Papaw said. "They don't seem to be paying no mind to..."

Mark froze with one foot out the door and on the gravels, but still holding Beth's hand.

"What? What's happening, Papaw?"

"A good many of them turned around just then, Mark. Staring right directly at us."

"Should we go?" Beth said. "The last thing I want is to get either one of you hurt."

"Exactly how do you think they could hurt us?" Clina said, laughing at the same time, but Mark still heard fear in her voice. "Every last one of us already passed over. That don't necessarily mean we can trust these folks."

"What do you want to do?" Mark said, watching Beth's eyes. Through all the strange things the two of them had experienced, he'd never seen a single reason not to trust her. And plenty of reason to heed what she and Clina said.

"If you think it's safe," Beth said, "we can at least walk around a little. Unlike our usual investigations, we shouldn't need respirators, right?"

He shrugged, welcoming the now-familiar discomfort mixed with excitement working its way through his mind and body. The predictable (and comparatively dull) routines of his bachelor life felt like a thousand years ago.

"Everything looked and smelled fine earlier. If nothing else, I do have our gear in the trunk. Wouldn't leave home with you without it."

She rolled her eyes and stepped out of the car.

As soon as she let go of his hand, Mark was surprised at how quiet their surroundings were. A bit of a breeze, a few birds twittering in the trees and scrub nearby. A faint whisper of the creek they were here to see. They were far enough away from the mine operations that he only smelled the autumn scents of dry leaves and soil, with sharp pine mixed in.

The grass and weeds alongside the road had recently been trimmed—probably for the inspection—creating a clearing in the midst of rough pine trunks and piles of gray boulders. The trimmed area still looked dusty and trampled from heavy boots passing through earlier.

He hadn't realized how noisy the mass of people in his Papaw's world had grown.

The second he touched Beth's hand again, he knew they'd gotten even louder on the other side.

"What's happening there?" Beth said.

"You're getting right close to the middle of the thing," Papaw said. "The line these people keep between themselves. Sounds to me like one bunch of them doesn't want us here."

"Okay, listen," Mark said. "I need the two of you to make me a promise. If they do figure out a way to hurt you, let us know so we can get out of here. For your sake, but for ours, too. We've met more than one ghost who could cause trouble for the living."

"Think I don't know that?" Clina snapped. "Happens to be how I met Beth and she met you, remember? Don't neither one of you worry 'bout us. We'll speak up should we need to."

"I won't let any of us come to harm, water bug," Papaw said. "Same as you'd do for me."

Beth pressed her full lips into a worried line, and Mark imagined he looked just as nervous.

"Let's get the basic gear just in case," she said, squeezing his hand. "Then lead the way."

CHAPTER 8

BETH TRIED NOT to let herself tense up too much, but it wasn't easy.

Knowing she and Mark were perfectly safe, that no one else should be nearby, and help would be around the next bend at the mine if anything actually happened didn't make much difference.

The constant low uproar in her mind rose and fell, but it never showed signs of stopping. The occasional raised voice ratcheted her tension up and never quite gave it a chance to relax.

She focused on the land around them while Mark got his own backpack out of the trunk and gathered their gear.

The slope beside the creek had the telltale smooth regularity of human contouring rather than the natural rumple of the mountains in the distance. Same with the thick grass and weeds surrounded by nothing but pine trees. She expected a nice bloom of so-called "wildflowers" would pop up every spring.

Very pretty and good for the local critters for sure. And every bit of it brought in from somewhere else as part of repairing the damage of mining. An improvement over the old days of leaving it a muddy mess, but not quite...natural.

She couldn't see the creek but she could hear it and smell the fresh water. The fact that it was regularly inspected at least kept her from worrying about the horrors of a place like Scatterland Creek.

"I think we might finally be getting through," Clina said. "Not sure if we done ourselves any favors."

The raspy laughter of Mark's Papaw rose above the increasing background noise.

"Turns out mentioning a few names did the trick. Maybe a little bit too well."

"What's wrong?" Beth said.

Mark paused, a small clear plastic respirator mask in hand. He reached out with the other to take Beth's.

"Nothing that ought to cause this much ruckus," Clina said. "Called out those two names is all, asking if we might could talk to them if they're close by. Whole dang crowd's running around acting a-fool now, like I tossed a great big stone into a mud puddle."

"Are they coming after you two?" Mark said.

"Naaaah, seem to have forgot we're even here," his Papaw said. "Can't tell if they're trying to find that Stanley and Hackworth, or trying to keep them hidden away. Either way, they sure are doing a whole lot of moving around that I can't see any sense in."

"How does the land look there?" Beth said. "Here everything is all rebuilt for big coal mines. Smoothed down and tamed, I guess you could call it."

"Not a thing out here but land stripped down bare of trees and most anything else that could grow," Clina said. "Like so much was in our time. Mud and rocks and mess as far as I can see, all up and down the sides of the mountains. Never has sprouted up and growed back healthy like it did around Bountyfield. Even around that nasty old Scatterland Creek, the land is sweet and growing again."

"Both sides got something that matters to them out here," Papaw said. "Otherwise they never would have followed us all this way outside town to such a dismal place."

Mark dropped the mask into his backpack and leaned against the car's trunk, still holding Beth's hand.

"I know I keep repeating myself, and I'll probably keep on doing it. If something is putting you at risk, let us know. We're going to walk toward the spot where I was earlier today, Papaw, when you said the trouble here was focused on me."

"Which means let us know if *Mark* is at risk, too," Beth said, scowling at him, only a little in jest. "Or if things seem to be getting worse for any reason."

"We sure will, Beth," his Papaw said. "From what I've come to know about you in such a short time, I expect you'd drag him back right quick if anything got too rough."

Beth stepped close to Mark, leaning against his chest with her arms around his shoulders. She'd shoved him out of the way of a falling rock only a week after they met, and dragged him backwards out of a toxic, stinking cave over the summer.

Walking him back along a creek should be nice and simple.

"Yes sir. I certainly would."

He kissed her long and hard, reminding her for a brief second that they hadn't come all the way up to Isom Gap to get involved in some kind of strange afterlife feud.

"This was supposed to be our vacation," she whispered. "A long-overdue one at that."

"Let's be more optimistic than that. We still have the weekend, right?"

"I like your idea much better. Okay, time to see who's after you and how hard I need to fight them off."

Mark smiled and kissed the tip of her nose, then turned back to the trunk when she stepped away. He handed her a compact black flashlight as he clipped an identical one to his belt.

He closed the trunk just as the noise in the afterlife got louder again. Beth held out her hand and faced toward the path.

"Sounds like we're not the only ones getting stirred up."

CHAPTER 9

THE CROWD NOISE on the other side was loud enough to make Mark's head ache before they went any distance, and Beth rubbed her temple with her free hand. Angry voices broke through the general roar, but he couldn't catch what they were saying.

A couple minutes walk up a gradual slope brought the creek into sight. Smaller versions of the boulders lined the channel, added as the mine operations grew to keep the waterway from flooding or drifting. The water danced and sparkled in the fading sunlight, running clean and perfectly clear.

No sign of the orange, red, or yellow of fouled mine runoff. No trace of sulfur stink, either. Only pine trees and fresh water.

His Papaw's shout rang uncomfortably clear.

"Here now! Get away from there!"

"We're going back," Mark said, letting Beth pull him that way.

"It's not you that's got 'em all stirred up," Clina said.

"We're the ones causing the trouble. More like giving it a place to roost."

The shouting intensified for a second, driving tension through Mark's shoulders and back. It was bad enough—more than bad enough—when he felt like something threatened Beth or Janie or anyone he cared about out in their world.

But here, where he couldn't even see, much less do anything about it, was a hundred times worse.

"Are we in the right place?" Beth said, trying to look everywhere at once.

"Don't think that matters no more," Clina said. "They're all overrun, both sides trying to push against the others. We got ourselves up on the hill and out of the way."

Beth looked at Mark with her eyebrows raised. Besides the gentle slope behind and a steeper tree-covered ridge ahead of them, the land was mostly level. Now.

"According to the mining plans," he said, "this area beside the road was flattened out a long time ago. To make moving the equipment easier."

The tone of his Papaw's next words brought him fiercely into Mark's mind, holding both of his big, rough hands up to try to calm a collection of his grandkids working themselves into an uproar.

Or among the adults if the gathering was on a holiday that involved drinking.

"I sure don't mean to argue with you, Clina Jane, but they don't look overrun to me. Least not on both sides. Seems to me like one side is trying to keep the other from getting through."

"Well," Clina said, drawling the word out. "I reckon you're right. They're trying to shove their way out now. That other bunch is doing everything they can to keep them from us."

"Trying to get through to what?" Beth said. "To you?"

"Maybe they finally turned up that Stanley boy," Clina said. "Him or the other one. Hackworth."

"Which side is trying to get through?" Mark said, remembering how this land and these operations had changed owners recently. His shadowy idea felt like a long-shot, but so did standing by a creek listening to crowds of brawling ghosts. "What direction?"

"They're toward the setting sun, water bug," Papaw said. "To the west no matter which side of the veil you're on."

Mark brought up the maps of the operation sites in his mind, watching the land features and contours shift around him. This creek split less than a quarter mile upstream.

"Let's go," Beth said before Mark drew breath to ask.

They started walking.

The crew that lined the waterway with rocks and boulders had left a nice wide space alongside, probably for maintenance as well as inspections. The weeds were only cleared for a few feet, but the footing was still good.

Nothing like the steep uphill hike to the lost miner's house pit, or the slippery stream bed along Scatterland Creek.

But Mark got the same deep sense of foreboding. The sensation of the world slipping out of true, away from what he'd always taken for reality with every step.

The shadows grew deeper as they went, with towering pines blocking out the fading traces of sunlight. Not quite dim enough for the flashlights just yet.

Absolutely perfect for Mark to imagine constant movement out of the corner of his eyes.

The growing din on Papaw and Clina's side of the world was almost enough to drown out the sounds of his and Beth's footsteps crunching through old leaves and spindly weeds.

"Which mine is on this land?" Beth said, reminding

Mark she'd met all the operators at lunch what felt like a long time ago. "The main guy, McConvey?"

"Not this part. His is farther on, the last drainage going into this creek. His loudmouth buddy Hackworth owns one side, and Denny Grissom the other."

"Grissom. He didn't say much of anything at lunch today. But he paid attention to everything."

"That's him. He's been around for years, like McConvey. Hackworth is the new kid in town. And he might have a family connection even he doesn't know about."

He drew breath to ask who she thought owned each side, but a deafening volley of shouts rang out in the other world.

"Calm yourselves down now!" Clina yelled. "We ain't going anywhere 'til you let them say their piece!"

"Papaw?"

"They're getting themselves all stirred up," he said. "Worse than before."

"Should we stop?" Beth said, looking into Mark's eyes. The blue in her own eyes looked black in the fading light.

"I think it's best to push on now that we got started," Clina said. "Someone in this bunch is right determined to get to us, and the other bunch just as bad wanting them to stop."

Mark unclipped his flashlight just as they came to the split in the creek. The main channel continued on but ran smaller, while the other branched off to the right.

To the west.

"We made it to the split," Mark said. "Any idea what they're trying—"

A scream cut through the cacophony on the other side, but not one voiced out of fear. This one sounded furious and determined. Another joined in, then another.

"Think we're about to find out," Papaw said. "Some of them just now broke through."

Mark and Beth followed the branch, close together on a much narrower path. Without a word, Beth focused her light on the ground in front of them, covered with a think coating of pine needles rather than weeds, while Mark watched the water for any changes.

The screaming drew closer, and it was everything Mark could do to keep walking. His ears and a big part of his mind were convinced they were heading right into the middle of a violent crowd.

Another surge of yells built up right behind the screamers. Clina raised her voice above it all.

"There comes the lot of them!"

The ground rumbled under their feet.

"What was that?" Beth said, shifting her tight grip to Mark's arm. "An *earthquake?*"

"Probably not, no." His mind reeled with too much fear and alarm to dig out the geological reasons. "That may be...it's possible something happened underground."

He hoped his voice didn't reflect how hard his heart pounded. With fear for the two of them, but more with terror for anyone working underground.

"In the mine," she whispered. "How many people are down there?"

"I don't think..."

Mark stopped, raising his head to sniff the wind like Janie would have done, but without her Redbone hound enthusiasm.

There was nothing pleasant or welcoming about that stink.

"What is it?" Beth said, pressing closer against him.

"Sulfur. First time I've caught scent of it out here." He ran the light ahead, and felt thuds like rocks falling into his belly. "See that? The streaks of yellow? Some kind of runoff is breaking through."

"Can't hear a dang one of you if everyone shouts at once!" Clina exclaimed. The noise died back for a second, then one woman yelled even louder.

"Ain't none of your business what goes on up here! You ran off and left a long damn time ago."

"That I did!" Clina shouted. "Best decision I ever made. That don't mean I'll stand by and let the likes of you shut me up!"

"The water's getting worse," Mark said, fighting his desire to pull Beth back from the spreading yellow-orange stain. "This won't make a bit of sense to anyone besides you, but that runoff cut through at the same time the people on the other side did. When the ground shook."

"Let me *be!*" a man shouted loud enough that Mark was more than half convinced it came from the world of the living. "We wasted more than enough time trying to reason with them. Now we got to take action while we still can!"

"Who owns this part?" Beth said. "Hackwork or Grissom?"

"It's...hang on, I need to call it in anyway, should have done that first thing. It's Hackworth, he bought it out a couple of years ago. McConvey's the emergency coordinator for this area though." He managed to clip the light back onto his belt, then pulled out his phone, hoping he could bring up the emergency reporting number with his hands shaking like crazy now. "The sensors underground should have let everyone know, but I need to, in case it was really bad."

"Clina, can you ask them what this is all about?" Beth said. "We're seeing something bad coming through in the water. And the ground shook just now, almost like an earthquake."

Mark and Beth flinched and huddled closer together when Clina hollered loud enough to punch right through the veil between their worlds.

"That's enough! All your fussing don't mean a *damn* to me, but you're causing trouble on both sides now!"

Mark's grandfather followed up—nowhere near as loud, but twice as furious.

"You're putting my family in danger. If they come to harm, I don't care how many you got bunched up together. You'll wish you could die all over again before I'm through with you."

The rowdy crowd settled down to surly muttering, and Mark wondered if any of them understood how seriously they should take that warning.

His Papaw was remarkably slow to anger.

But once it happened, no one ever forgot.

"Now put your heads together and pick out someone to tell me what's got you all tore up," Clina said. "And don't think I'll put up with a bunch of you running your mouths at the same time."

Mark almost dropped his phone when it buzzed in his hand, but he blew out a relieved breath when he read the message.

McConvey, all business and concern, like anyone should be at a time like this. No injuries, no rockfalls, no explosions. Everyone evacuating from all the operating mines in the area right now, investigation already underway.

He held it up for Beth to read before tapping out a reply. Turned out concentrating on a text message was a challenge with two angry ghost mobs struggling to pick their leaders inside his mind.

Still onsite, no injuries. Felt the shake here. Seeing likely runoff in creek on Hackworth side. Will need word from him on storage sites underground.

The water still carried a thick streak of discoloration when Mark checked, but the reek of sulfur wasn't any stronger.

"Should we stay here?" Beth said, training her own light upstream. "In case the runoff gets worse?"

Mark shook his head, trying to find a logical course in a most illogical situation.

"That wouldn't be a bad idea, but not for the obvious reasons. If that shake *was* caused by a spectral fighting match of some kind, we might at least be able to...I don't know, warn somebody before it gets worse?"

Beth snorted out a laugh, and Mark saw her adorable blush even by the flashlight. She pulled him toward a couple of the larger boulders, close enough to see but not get a lungful from the newly fouled creek.

"The things you do for the Commonwealth of Virginia. Let's get comfortable if we're going to be referees for the afterlife."

CHAPTER 10

BETH PULLED Mark down to the rock beside her, not wanting to admit how she really felt in that moment.

If she could do anything to prevent it, she would not let him go underground here. Not right after some kind of quake or roof fall or even an explosion, for certain.

Investigating that kind of potential disaster wasn't his job, and she didn't need to remind him that he wasn't all that well trained for it.

The biggest reason was if the angry ghost crowd on other side *had* managed to punch through somehow—to shake the ground and possibly alter the groundwater—they might be able to do worse. Especially now that they were so agitated and stirred up.

And they'd been trying to get to Mark when he was out here earlier. Letting him take himself closer to an unknown danger that was *targeting* him felt like far beyond what she could tolerate.

Of course he was a grown-ass man and could take good care of himself. He had for thirty-six years before he met her.

None of that changed how she felt.

The people around Clina returned to arguing and shouting, and pushing and shoving hard enough that Beth heard that part too.

She let out a slow breath and leaned against Mark's shoulder, staring up at the faint wash of stars overhead. An orange glow from the west faded most of them out. The clearest evidence of Hackworth's operation being so close by.

Well, the clearest besides the ground shaking under their feet and the foul streak in the water that she smelled now. Like a convention of perturbed skunks were passing by just out of sight.

"What could make water leak out like that all at once?" she said.

She heard a smile in his voice, at first.

"You mean besides the obvious and scientific answer of angry ghosts hanging out nearby? If there's some kind of buildup in one of the chambers, a shake like that might have shifted the rock enough to let water slip through. But there's not supposed to be any kind of water storage right there, groundwater or wastewater or anything else. Not on any of the maps I've seen."

"Then what else could cause it? Aside from Clina's ghosts full of piss and vinegar. And sulfur."

He shook his head and the muscles in his shoulder moved as he shrugged. She welcomed the warmth when he put his arm around her.

"It could be an undetected buildup, kind of like what we ran into at Scatterland Creek with all the rain and snow this spring. That doesn't seem likely here though, with no history of that kind of problem. Or…"

He paused, and this time she felt his chest rise and fall with a slow breath.

"Or?"

"Or they're illegally storing wastewater there without letting anyone know. Again, nothing like that has happened out here before, not on my watch at least. It's not unknown elsewhere. If an operator can't afford to handle the wastewater safely underground or aboveground, or they just don't want to pay. A huge part of the problem is if the site isn't set up to be watertight, it can be a lot worse than a trickle like this. Not that this isn't bad enough."

They listened to the argument on the other side, not quite as loud but showing no signs of slowing just yet.

And no signs of rising loud and harsh enough to cause another rumble under their feet.

"Based on what you know of Hackworth, do you think he would actually do something like that?"

Mark leaned his head to the left and right, then let it fall forward toward his chest.

"I don't know. No, that's not right. I don't *think* he would, I really don't. Like I said before, he's the new kid in town, or at least the newer one. But as much trouble as he talks with McConvey, he's never shown any signs of actually getting angry with me, or pushing back. He follows the laws and regulations and complains the whole time like most. And, most people who intend to cause trouble don't buddy up with a grouchy-ass straight arrow like McConvey, you know? It doesn't feel right to me."

"Clina and Papaw, did either of you get a feeling about the folks we had lunch with? Hackworth or McConvey, or the others? Like you did about Deborah Fleming?"

"Can't say I caught anything off about them," Mark's Papaw said slowly, raising his voice against the ongoing mutters. "Most seemed like a regular rowdy bunch of working folks."

"Wait, something *was* off about Deborah Fleming?" Mark said. "The one who brought that photo to Beth?"

"She put me in mind of that one that helped you a few months back," Clina said. "Melanie I think her name was. Had the same feel of being hounded by the shadow of her family, wanting some way to let light get to her instead of all that dark. Going by what we're seeing here, Deborah's shadows have got thick as tar."

Beth shivered at the image of oily, low-hanging clouds following someone around all the days of her life. No wonder Deborah seemed a little twitchy.

"Going by the way Susan fired up when she saw that picture," Beth said, "she'll have all the names verified by in the morning and all the missing ones puzzled out not long after. But I'd go with our inside sources on this one no matter what she turns up."

"This is going to sound strange, even for the situation. I was thinking earlier that it sounded like Clina and Papaw were mad enough to punch right through the veil. That put me more in mind of what happened to you over in Estonoa more than I want to admit."

The gears in Beth's mind spun for a second before they found traction.

She wished they'd just kept slipping.

"You mean the way the plague of sinner moths broke through. That was our world cracking into theirs, but you're right. There's no reason it couldn't go the other way. Or maybe both at the same time, and let more than ghost critters get out."

"I don't know what a flood of poisonous mine wastewater would do over there," he said. "Or how a backlog of bad feelings would hit either side. I truly don't want to find out. We may have to figure out how to fix this one from both sides at the same time."

"We have to figure out how to find it first. What worries me now is even if we can find it, what the hell are we going to do about it?"

The ghostly world turned the volume from mutter to uproar as she spoke.

CHAPTER 11

THE ROCK WAS cold underneath his legs and backside, but Mark couldn't exactly say he minded sitting with his arm around Beth and her snuggled close to keep them both warm. No matter how strange the circumstances.

The noise level in his Papaw's world rose one more time, then dropped down to whispers and what sounded like shuffling feet. A young man's voice spoke up clear and confident, but with undertones of anger.

"No one here can speak of this thing more'n me, cause ain't no one lost as much as me. No matter what else they might try to tell you." A resentful chorus whispered like wind through the trees, then died down. "Name's Jacob Stanley in case you don't already know out there on the other side. I'm the one that died and started off all this nonsense."

"Show me a Stanley ever to tell the truth," a woman's voice shouted. "I'll show you a Hackworth knows better from the minute they're born."

"This is the old feud you told me about?" Mark said. "And they're literally carrying it beyond the grave?"

"Gettin' the idea why I left this place?" Clina said. "Folks here stay spiteful even after they're long in the ground. And here you two drag me back right into the middle of this mess."

"What's that got to do with the ground shaking on the other side?" Papaw said. "And the fouled water? Gotta say that don't quite sit right in my mind."

"Not a blamed thing, Mary Hackworth," Jacob Stanley said. "Not unless you count all that mess of poison stored up under the ground. Trying to destroy our home and harm ones that don't deserve it all over again."

"Only harm done was to Purvis Lee Hackworth!" Mary shouted back. "Had to move off far away from here or he'd tell you so his damn self!"

Mark's blood ran cold at the idea of something underground that might be leaking out.

"Wait, this won't help us or them," he said. "Papaw, we have to know what he meant, what's building up there. Why it's breaking loose. Otherwise we might have real trouble in both places."

"All right, now listen," Papaw said, and Mark knew he again held his hands out in that soothing gesture. "I expect everyone here already knows about the bad blood between your families from a long way back, and a great many of you will jump at the chance to tell me and Clina all about it. What I got to know about right now is that earth shake. A whole lot more folks stand to suffer if that keeps up."

Mark's phone buzzed with another message from McConvey.

Hackworth swears no waste stored underground, not anywhere onsite. Swears the mine is dry. No records of that kind of trouble there. Investigators still working, looking for your runoff, possible source of the shake. Grissom and Harrison on the way in. Keep me updated.

Mark strained to hear into the near-silence in the world coming to him through Beth's touch. His Papaw spoke again.

"Listen, son, I know you're upset. Looks to me like you were just a boy when you passed. Doubt you ever got to the far side of fifteen. That's a damn shame." He paused. "I'm real sorry for your loss too, Miss Hackworth. I've had someone I care for move far away, and I know how bad that hurts. What you can both do is help us stop a whole bunch more getting hurt."

"That's the very reason I ran up here so hard," Jacob Stanley said, silencing a wave of whispers and mutters. "To stop the wrong that's being done, all the bad piling up where it don't belong for year upon year and no sign of stopping. I pushed...I pushed with all I got to get through to you. To the other side. Never knew I could cause trouble for the living, and I'm sorry for that. But once I felt someone there, I had to get help no matter what."

"Do you think something happening here could make the poison worse there?" Mark said, pausing for his Papaw to repeat the words. "Something where it's not supposed to be? My Papaw's right, a whole lot more folks could come to trouble over this. You were right to reach out, Jacob. Let us help stop it."

"We don't *know* what made it get worse," Mary Hackworth said. "Or why. Showed up here as a dead space on the mountain. Gray and dead. Nothing wild nor tame grows there, and no kind of animal goes in. I thought...well, no one thought it come from the world of living folks. Never have heard of such a thing as that."

"Might you point it out to us, Mary?" Clina said, her tone soothing. "Been gone from here a long time, with my own reasons. But I'll not stand by and let harm rain down when I can stop it. Fighting to stop death from under the ground is what let me get through to the other side. My

73

friends *are* living. Got a real knack for trouble, truth be told, always getting up to something. But they work real hard to make things better, too."

Mark tried not to hold his breath. Even if the long-gone residents of Isom Gap could put aside their feud long enough to make the attempt, the dead spot there might not join up to whatever was happening around him and Beth.

The tension of her body matched his own.

"She's pointing to the northwest, water bug," Papaw said. "Looks close by where you are."

"Toward where this creek starts higher up. But it doesn't match the mining operations. At least not the maps I've seen." He froze, staring upstream, fitting the topographic map in his head with what his eyes saw. "If there's something new, natural or manmade, the investigation crew won't know about it. It's not on any of the maps. They could tunnel right into the source of the runoff."

He grabbed for his phone, dialing McConvey's number rather than taking time for a text.

"McConvey here. Better be good, Mr. Hersch."

"Listen, have you got investigators on the border between Hackworth and Grissom's operations?"

"All due respect to you, but where the hell else do you think I should have them? You're the one saying there's runoff in that stream, not me."

Mark got up to pace, scrubbing one hand through his hair. For once he didn't mind stepping away from Beth if it meant temporarily losing his connection to the dead.

"Get them out of there, Mr. McConvey. From what I'm seeing here, I suspect there's a flooded chamber that's not on the maps. If there's enough to break through into the creek, the inspectors could flood the whole mine before they know what hit them."

Beth stood beside Mark, but she didn't touch him.

McConvey tapped on the back of his phone loud enough that Mark heard it.

"Okay, Mr. Hersch. I'll pull them back. I sure do hope you can show us where this supposedly unknown chamber is before it rumbles more water loose."

"I'll do my best. Can you get me inside right now?"

"Mark, no," Beth said, stepping into his arms. "Let them clear it out first."

He held the phone against his chest. "If I can work with both sides at once somehow, I'll have a chance of pinning it down. Otherwise they could wander around for a long time searching. Some of these mines are huge, and over a century old."

He felt her shaking her head against his shoulder.

But she didn't *say* no.

"Sorry about that, Mr. McConvey. Didn't catch what you said."

"I'm at the entrance myself, not far from where you are at that creek. Waiting on Grissom. Get yourself here in five minutes and I'll see what I can do. No promises."

"Just pull the investigators, please. I'll be right there."

Beth stepped back, still shaking her head, but she held onto his hand.

"Clina, can you two make sure they don't cause any more shakes? Mark is going to try to find out where this dead spot is on our side."

"And stop it from getting worse," Mark said.

"They seem a good bit more quiet than they were," Clina said. "Not near so full of piss and vinegar."

"I think they remember how bad the logging was," Papaw said. "And the mining that came after. How bad it scarred up the land. This young man wasn't the only one who lost his life. If you can stop that kind of thing happening again, they prob'ly still won't get along too well. But they'll do right by the rest of us."

"Good enough for me," Mark said. But he wasn't sure it was good enough for Beth. "I'm sorry, sweetheart. If there's some kind of unknown flooded chamber and it's leaking, it could already be too unstable to leave alone. I have to go see."

Beth stepped back and threw both hands up, jabbing the beam of her flashlight into the pine trees overhead.

"I know you do, Mark. I was in that lost mine with you, and closer to that Bountyfield cave than I wanted to be. I'll go in this mine with you too. You know you can't hear a thing from across the veil without me. Let's go."

Mark reached for her free hand, his heart and gut clenched with what he had to say, even though he had no other choice.

"Wait. I feel like an ass saying this, but you can't go with me. At least not into the mine."

She pulled free of his hand and planted both of hers on her hips.

"Exactly what do you think you can do to stop me? I'm not exactly some kind of fragile damsel in need of rescue, you know. I can *more* than hold my own."

Mark winced. He didn't blame her one bit for being upset, but Beth getting hurt while she protected him days after they first met was hardly his favorite memory.

"It's not *me* doing anything. You can't just walk into a working mine under the best of circumstances, not even I or any other inspector can do that. This mine's on emergency status right now. The state would tan my hide if I took you inside. They'd take care of McConvey, Hackworth, and Grissom for good measure, and anyone else who didn't stop you."

Beth scowled, but he knew by the way her mouth and chin quivered that she believed him.

He'd never once in all his life been foolish enough to misunderstand an angry woman's tears.

"That's not..." She blinked and looked away. "Then what am I supposed to do? What are *you* supposed to do, Mark? You can't hear Clina or anyone on the other side by yourself."

He covered his mouth with one hand, shaking his head. That hadn't yet crossed his mind. And the only reason for him to get involved in this potential disaster at all was his ability to find the problem his Papaw could see.

Beth was right. He couldn't hear any of the ghosts without touching her.

Except...

"I hadn't thought about this since the day it happened," he said, "but I could hear the lost miner on my own that day. Remember? Before we even went inside. I couldn't hear Clina, and I haven't heard anyone else on my own. But I *did* hear him."

Beth took a deep breath, held it for a second, then let it out in a rush. She grabbed his hand and took a step down the path to his car.

"I do remember that. Come on, let's get going, we'll talk in the car. I don't want McConvey to go in without you."

Mark followed, a little weak-kneed at her quick under-standing, and a hell of a lot grateful for everything about her.

"Okay," she said. "The last thing we'd want to do is recreate a situation that desperate, assuming that's what let him get through to you. When did you hear him?"

"As soon as I touched the glass plate negative. After that I heard him until we carried him out of the mine. Not at all since then."

"So it was touch, just like with me. And it may have been because he was so lonesome and miserable. We don't have anything like that with us, unless this works for you without me."

She stopped walking, held her flashlight under her arm, and slipped the copper chain over her head. The thumb-sized bit of glass flashed as it passed through the light's sideways beam.

"Clina, can you do me a favor?" she said. "Count to five, then say something to Mark. Then please ask Papaw to do the same. We need to figure out if he can hear you without me touching him."

She dropped the necklace into Mark's hand without waiting for an answer. He closed his fingers around it, still warm from her body.

He closed his eyes, too, concentrating all his attention on how that ghostly world sounded and felt to him. He listened so hard that he heard his own heartbeat in the otherwise quiet evening.

Beth wrapped her hands around his, and he heard his Papaw at once.

"...think he can hear me at all, Beth. I'm real sorry."

"That's okay, Papaw," Mark said, looking into Beth's eyes. "We'll just have to figure out something else."

"I counted to ten after you had the necklace," she said. "I don't know what to do. If we had a picture of him, maybe, or something of his. But everything is back in Bountyfield."

When she moved to put the necklace back on, Mark's eyes went to another flash in the light.

More of a sparkle than a bit of antique glass could throw off.

"I might have an idea. There's no polite way to put this, and we're not exactly in a normal situation, so I'll just be blunt. Can I take a look at your ring?"

Beth stared at him for a second, brows knotted, before her eyes went wide.

"Yes! That's a great idea." She pulled her placeholder engagement ring off and slipped it onto his pinky finger. "Okay, Papaw. Do your very best to say something to Mark. Clina, maybe you can help him somehow?"

At first, in the silence, Mark thought they were out of options, and he'd be wandering around in the vast, likely dangerous mine as clueless as McConvey's men. But only he would know they were running out of time on both sides of the divide.

Then a strange, slow whisper started up what sounded like miles away, and gradually grew louder. He concentrated again, so hard he squeezed his hands into fists.

"...hear me, Mark? I'm right here, water bug."

"I hear you! Really soft and quiet, but you're there."

Beth grinned and held her fists up in a victory sign.

"Fantastic! Okay, now we really have to get going. Keep talking, see if you can make it stronger. Clina says she can't hear a word, but she feels like someone new is close by."

They walked faster this time, but Mark didn't lose one bit of his sense of wonder.

"Is everyone still calm there?" he said.

The words came through a bit louder, and he could tell Papaw was raising his voice.

"Milling around like a bunch of lost sheep without a good dog to point 'em in the right direction. Some gathering up around that dead spot."

"We're heading to the mine as fast as we can. Beth, do you think you should come back here? If we get separated by too much, can we still talk?"

"Clina says she can still hear people back in Bountyfield, but it's faint like you said. It might make sense for me to come back either way, so I can keep an eye on the creek."

They got into the car, and Mark kept what were surely minor worries about Beth sitting out in the nighttime woods by herself to himself. No more than remnants of all his years of city living, especially compared with what could potentially go wrong where he was going.

"Can you hear me, Beth? In your mind, I mean?"

"I don't think so. It might work better once we're closer to home."

Mark hesitated as he navigated the gravel road and turned onto the main one, following the steady climb toward the mine entrance. Outside of town and even as high as Isom Gap already was, the quick elevation gain of over a thousand feet would likely make him have to clear his ears again.

He couldn't deny one question would bother him if he didn't ask. Being distracted while underground was never a good idea.

He kept his voice as low as he could, even though he wasn't sure why.

"Papaw, have you ever seen or heard of Granny there? Since the last time I asked you, I mean."

They'd talked about this before, how Mark's grandmother had never shown up on the other side even though she was buried right beside his grandfather in Bountyfield. Clina said sometimes people seemed to get lost along the way. For days or months, and in a few cases, years later, they would show up like not a day had passed.

Sometimes they never showed up at all.

"Never have heard a whisper from her or about her, Mark. I sure do wish I would. Getting to talk to you makes missing her a lot easier."

Mark kept his next thoughts to himself. His curiosity about whether communicating through his Granny's ring might someday help her find her way to the other side after all.

Right now he had to focus on doing everything he could

to keep a lot of souls on the side of the living where they belonged.

Misunderstanding his quiet, Beth reached over and stroked his cheek above his beard, letting the rising and falling voices of Isom Gap's ghosts filter into his mind.

"It's going to be okay, Mark. We'll figure it out together."

CHAPTER 12

THE BLINDING bright lights outside the mine entrance surprised Beth, along with the startling number of people moving around.

A long, low building stood off to the side, made of green-painted steel with what looked like a bunch of garage doors along the front. Almost all of them stood open, revealing big mining machines she didn't know the names for.

No one was paying attention to anything inside the machine shop, though.

At least fifty people gathered around an arched entrance cut into the hillside and lined with metal. That's where the spotlights came from too, all around the entrance. Huge blue metal pipes that she knew were ventilation fans—easily ten feet tall—extended along the ground and away from the entrance on either side.

Several people wore the dark blue coveralls of coal miners, the orange and silver reflective stripes around their legs, arms, and chests glowing like gigantic fireflies. Even from fifty yards away, Beth saw soot-colored grime around their faces and necks, with pale, owlish circles around their eyes, mouths, and noses.

A bunch more who weren't quite so covered with coal dust wore regular coveralls that were plenty stained, probably from working in the deserted machine shop.

Both groups were mostly men, but she saw more women than she expected.

A handful wore street clothes, mostly blue jeans. Beth recognized the operators they'd had lunch with among them. They gathered close to the machine shop building around a blocky, low vehicle she didn't recognize.

Mark parked in a wide graveled lot across from the building, full of mostly pickup trucks even at this hour. The tendons in his hands stood out when he squeezed the steering wheel for a second before he turned to her.

"I'm sorry about having to leave you out here, Beth. I don't much want to go in myself, but I feel like one of us has to."

She pressed her forehead against his shoulder, then ran her hand along the back of his. He finally relaxed his grip and linked his fingers through hers.

"I don't love any of this, either. But I do love you. Remember what you said to Clina and Papaw? That we'd get away if anything is too dangerous for them? You need to do the same. If it gets bad, get yourself out however you have to. Got it?"

He held her hand against his lips and nodded.

"Got it. Come with me to talk to them? I can hear Papaw a little, but you can hear the whole ghost convention going on around here. You might be able to catch something I miss."

Beth raised one eyebrow. "Of course I'm going with you. That wasn't up for negotiation."

When he let go to get out, she touched her necklace

through his old t-shirt. The restless chatter had died down from constant arguments to more of an intense discussion.

"Anything changed there? Since we moved to a different place?"

"Got one side stubbed up and refusing to say a damn word," Clina said. "Staying out of the way at least. Me and Walt got right up on that dead spot, watching the rest talk it over."

Beth joined Mark at the front of the car and took his hand so he could hear more clearly. With the roar of the powerful fans, it was hard to hear much of anything else.

The smell of diesel hung oily in the air, making her think too much of the clouds of family trouble plaguing Deborah Fleming.

"Never seen anything quite like it," Papaw said. "Grass and leaves crisped up and black as charcoal, but not a trace of ashes or any kind of burned smell. More like…something dead. Rotten."

Mark lowered his voice as they got closer to the people milling around near the entrance. Now Beth could see a series of lights stretching inside the opening in two lines overhead and two along the bottom of the tunnel.

"Be careful there, both of you," he said. "Already passed on or not, whatever that is can't be safe. Does it smell like sulfur? Like rotten eggs, Papaw? Or a skunk?"

"No, I can't say it does, water bug. More like an animal knocked off to the side of the road and bloated up in the sun for a couple days."

"All the more reason to stay back," Mark said. "I'm going into the mine now, so I'll need you to guide me as much as you can. Beth is going back to the creek. That way we might have a chance of getting at this thing from both sides."

Mark's Papaw sighed long and hard enough that Beth heard it.

"All that good advice you give us, Mark? About keeping ourselves safe and out of harm's way? I might not need to say that goes more than double for you under the ground in that mine, but I will. Watch out for yourself, hear me? Both of you."

Mark stopped far enough away that none of the operators would be able to hear him and pulled Beth into a quick hug.

"We will, Papaw," he said close against her ear. "I promise."

"We sure will," Beth said, gritting her teeth to keep any tears from making it from her throat to her eyes.

Bill McConvey stood with his hands jammed onto his hips, not quite yelling at one of the men wearing the reflective miner's coveralls. Beth noticed Chip Hackworth watching from off to the side, shirt half-untucked from his jeans, brown hair a frazzled mess.

"Didn't you say this is Hackworth's operation?" she whispered.

"On paper," Mark said under his breath. "In reality most of the time. Not surprised to see this change tonight. I'm sure McConvey sees Hackworth as someone brand new who hasn't earned his trust yet."

McConvey glanced up, saw Mark, and changed the direction of his rapid-fire words.

"Thought I told you five minutes, Mr. Hersch. Just about missed your chance here, assuming you still want to take it. Get your ass suited up or get back and stay out of the way."

"Pipe the hell down, Bill," a woman's voice said from behind Beth. They turned to see Lisa Harrison directing a death glare toward McConvey. "I don't see your gear materializing out of thin air just yet. And last I heard, you weren't the expert in water quality and management, which is what we need right this minute. We're damn lucky Mark is here, and that he's willing to try and help. Not to mention this being *Hackworth's* site, not yours last time I checked."

McConvey turned his head to the side, mouth tight, but he never even met Lisa's eyes. He waved one hand toward the machine shop.

"Go on, then. You too, Hackworth. The mantrips under the ground here can carry eight, so you might as well come along too, Grissom. Lisa, you planning to jump in and drive, maybe direct us once we get underground, too?"

Lisa flashed a sweet smile that Beth recognized all too well. That smile and the words that followed would draw blood if you brushed up against them the wrong way.

"Why no, Bill, I don't think I will. You might want to remember my job is on the surface in a situation like this. I reckon I'll stay up here and make sure things are under control on this side. That way if you need a rescue yourself, you'll have someone competent to handle it."

Clina's chuckle matched how Beth felt perfectly. McConvey snorted and shook his head.

"Suit yourself. That's Hackworth's call to make, as you so helpfully pointed out. Not mine."

Mark spoke before everyone headed toward the machine shop and their gear.

"Beth is going back over to the creek to keep an eye out for more runoff. I've got an idea where we need to aim compared to where we were when the runoff started. Mr. Hackworth, mind if she takes one of your radios along?"

Hackworth's pale face flushed red, and Beth was certain he was forcing himself not to look to McConvey for an answer. Hackworth nodded, but didn't say a word. Once again, Lisa stepped forward.

"How about this. I'll go with Beth, and with a radio. Then we'll be able to let you know if anything else happens." She turned to Beth. "You felt that shake out there, right?"

"We did. Just a minute or so before the yellow boy showed up in the creek."

Lisa smiled at the correct slang term for the discoloration in the water.

"Sounds like we have a plan, gentlemen."

Mark winked at Beth, then walked off with Hackworth and Grissom. McConvey nodded once at Lisa before he followed.

"Don't pay any attention to Bill," Lisa said. "I promise you he shit his pants first thing before he realized it wasn't *his* mine having the problem."

Beth let out a breath through her lips, watching Mark step into a bright orange pair of coveralls, the reflective stripes flashing silver.

"You don't think it could be from his mine?" she said. "Or from Grissom's?"

Lisa held up one hand and tilted it back and forth.

"From where that creek is, the runoff could be from any of them. That's one reason I want to see where the trouble is for myself. Give us a better idea where it could be coming from. We'll have to radio back to someone on the surface here, then they'll communicate to underground. You doing okay?"

Beth started to say of course she was, but something in Lisa's voice caught her attention.

This was not someone who didn't understand everything that could go wrong here. Lisa knew exactly what she was asking, and why.

"I'm hanging in there," Beth said. "I don't much like Mark going underground when they have no idea what's happening."

Lisa nodded, and her eyes were sympathetic.

"Makes sense. You two haven't been together all that long, right? And he's usually out splashing through creeks and streams instead of putting on a hardhat."

"Right on both counts. I appreciate you going back out there with me."

By the time Beth and Lisa got to the shop, everyone was suited up. Hackworth held out a black rectangle of red and green blinking electronics about the size of a soda can toward Lisa.

Beth had only been around him for a couple of hours, but she already knew his quiet, serious demeanor was unusual to say the least.

"Thanks, Lisa," he said. "Got someone assigned to stand by out here and listen out for you."

"Good deal, Chip. First time with an incident for you, if I remember right."

He closed his eyes for a second and nodded.

"I'm just glad we got the crews out with no trouble. I got all my training in mind, don't worry."

He walked toward McConvey, who again stood with his hands hard on his hips, talking at Grissom this time.

"Chip just had his first hands-on mine rescue training as an operator," Lisa said. "He did good, but I don't think he expected to be putting it into use quite this soon. I'll let you speak to Mark now. Meet you in the parking lot."

Beth turned to see Mark, coveralls and hardhat on, clear plastic respirator in hand, matching safety glasses tucked into his breast pocket. He had on gloves, too, giving him protection and cover for the strange reality of a diamond engagement ring on his pinky.

"What are they saying?" Beth said. "About conditions inside?"

"No signs of instability in the roof. Not a trace of anything like an aftershock. Not a drop of water that wasn't there before, either, not where they're looking at least. Much to my surprise, they're willing to go where I suggested." He stepped closer, pulled one glove off, and reached for her hand. "What are *they* saying?"

"Mostly saying whatever it is to each other," Clina said. "Only this young man Jacob Stanley here wants a thing to do with us. Says he never did feel safe speaking out about that dead place growing 'til he caught on to you, Mark."

"No pressure there, then," Mark said, reaching up to stroke Beth's cheek. "I'll do my best to help him, and I hope he'll let me know if I'm about to get all of us into trouble."

Beth returned his gentle kiss, wishing all over again that their evening together hadn't been hijacked.

Even though she knew in her bones that neither one of them would turn their backs on the living or the dead.

"You better get going before McConvey decides to yell at both of us. Get back to me as fast as you can."

"I'll be back here getting on your nerves again before you even know I'm gone."

CHAPTER 13

MARK'S CONFIDENCE was shaken considerably by leaving Beth's side and having to step right into a massive freight elevator with McConvey, Hackworth, Grissom, and a senior miner who would drive them deep into the mine itself.

Exploring natural caves or even mines he could walk himself into was one thing, and one of his favorite things to do. But putting himself at the mercy of so much machinery and into places dug and blasted out of the guts of a mountain always put him on edge.

He never could shake the sense that the mountain resented the intrusion. And therefore would do everything possible to regain her own domain and privacy and close up that access forever. No matter what violence to the intruders took place in the process.

The drop of the elevator—what looked like an open-sided bare metal box liberally stained with coal dust—reminded him way too much of falling over a cliff edge.

Then the ride in a mantrip: a just-past-waist-high vehicle broad and long enough to carry eight miners and their equipment, only carrying half that tonight. Mark didn't especially enjoy the way the seat sloped back at a sharp angle to keep the clearance low for short passages in the mine, but it was worth it to have a steel roof over his head.

Unlike several of the mantrips he'd ridden in, this one rolled on rubber tires rather than being confined to rails along the mine's floor. The mine itself—what he saw of it at first—looked like a narrow, low highway tunnel, if highway tunnels were white and had bundles of cables and thick ventilation shafts running overhead.

Not to mention well-lit enough that a car's headlights would have been useless, with bright fixtures at regular intervals overhead.

It was fairly clean, too, with Hackworth's crew doing as good a job as any of the operators he'd met with today. The squared-off tunnel had been sprayed down with white rock dust mixed with water to cut down on possibly explosive coal dust, and no drifts of spilled coal or little rockfalls piled up in the corners.

Even with the mine eerily empty and still after the shake, it was obvious the miners took as much pride in this operation as Hackworth did.

Along the way toward the part of the mine nearest the creek, big chambers opened up on either side. The active rooms better lit than the older ones if the typical pattern held. The room-and-pillar approach left more square corridors as the coal and rock were removed in sections, leaving blocky support pillars behind.

Only faint scents—like damp gravels and faint chemical additives from dried rock dust—lingered in the dry air with the whole mine shut down. Cool fresh air from outside blown in by massive fans kept the temperature low.

The mantrip's quiet electric motor only emphasized the unusual silence.

Much as he preferred to spend time in the open air along

waterways, Mark was endlessly fascinated with the way these big operations worked. And he never forgot how dangerous they were, inside and out. All the tech and planning and safety measures helped, sure, as did things like the rows of steel roof plates they rode under right now.

But the risks of the mine and the job itself endured.

He managed not to jump for a change when a disembodied voice spoke up inside his head.

"Me and Clina are keeping 'em calm, water bug. Like she said before, that poor Stanley boy, Jacob, he's been scared and worried about that dead spot for a long time. Never could get a soul to listen to him. He's convinced he recognized it since it started up on account of the way he passed. Says he started trying to reach out to us as soon as we got to Isom Gap. First time he felt like he might get through. Focused on *you* to tell you the truth. Prob'ly why you got so jumpy out by that creek today."

Mark glanced at Denny Grissom in the sharply reclined seat beside him, head leaned back, eyes closed. Tense lines around his mouth and forehead dispelled any notion that he could actually be asleep.

Sending a silent thanks to Hackworth and his loan of gray safety gloves, Mark ran his thumb along the lump of his grandmother's ring, turned to the inside of his pinky finger. Trying to explain why he was wearing a diamond engagement ring to this bunch was stress he truly didn't need in that moment.

He turned away to stare at the chambers passing by.

"That might be how the runoff got out into that stream," he whispered. "If he had to push trying to get through. We've seen more than once how your world can affect ours. I just have to figure out where it is and how the hell it got there. Any way to tell *when* the dead spot got so much worse? I sure would like to get an idea of how much water we may be up against before we accidentally break through."

His grandfather's calm words talking to someone else made more noise than the mine as the mantrip slowed, then turned down a short corridor to the left.

"I'm sorry to say that one's an awful lot harder to answer, Mark. Before Clina got through to Beth and brought me through to you, it was near impossible to know how the time was passing. If a new soul showed up we got an idea, sure. Unless they were just too confused to know like happens sometimes. But that was in years, or even decades. Something like days or weeks, that's near impossible to say."

"Kind of hard to keep track of the seasons too, I guess."

The mantrip slowed as they passed over a rough spot on the floor, jolting everyone inside. From what Mark knew of the way the mine was laid out, they were getting close to the edge where the water had to be.

If it was there at all.

"Don't be so sure about not knowing the seasons," Papaw said. "We get the changes from warm to cold just like you do. We had a hard, rough winter, same as you did in Bountyfield. About all young Stanley could pin down is the trouble got worse after all that snow melted."

Mark gripped the steel bar beside him. Assuming he already knew the answer in a situation like this could do a lot more than send him down the wrong path.

Whatever was happening was already causing trouble in the ghostly world.

It could prove deadly to those who hadn't yet passed over.

"You mean when we had all kinds of extra water," he said. "The exact thing that caused the flooding we ran into at Scatterland Creek. In a cave that never flooded before this year."

The mantrip slowed to a stop parallel to a solid wall of

rock butted up against another wall at a near-perfect right angle. Mark made sure his safety glasses were firmly in place, then pulled himself up out of the low-slung seat and joined the others standing near the corner. With only the low roar of the massive ventilation fans, none of them wore the hearing protection required by rock-chewing machinery and yelling miners.

Much as he wanted to find out what was going on, he envied the driver staying beside the vehicle, radio in hand.

McConvey leaned against the rock face and crossed his arms, but for once he didn't say a word. He only stared daggers at Hackworth, who was also uncharacteristically quiet.

"Where did you have in mind, Mr. Hersch?" Hackworth finally said.

McConvey rolled his eyes, but Mark ignored him and walked close to the wall. He caught a strong scent of wet rock, but no sulfur or anything else strange.

"According to the maps I've seen, this rock face runs above the creek where we felt the shake. Have you seen any kind of water buildup in the lower chambers, Mr. Hackworth? Anything that might indicate trouble up here?"

Hackworth tipped his white hardhat up enough to scratch his head.

"Haven't seen or heard of anything like that, no. The water pumps in the lower levels keep everything drained like always. Have seen a few strange things in this room, though. The sensors on this level? They picked up that shake you're talking about. We thought for sure we'd find the roof slipped. Not a scrap of that, either. And none of the sensors on other levels caught the shake."

The hair on Mark's arms tried to stand up under his jacket and the heavy coveralls. Even though he'd seen evidence of the ghosts affecting the world of the living more than once, and in spectacular fashion, part of him was still amazed at what they could do.

"That's not exactly what we'd expect with something I felt so clearly above ground, is it?" He took several steps away from the corner, brushing his gloved fingers along the wall, willing his Papaw to guide him.

"Well, no," Hackworth said, glancing at McConvey again. "I can't exactly explain that one myself."

"Bothered to check your other sensors lately?" McConvey said. "Run a test on your whole system? Got to do that from time to time, you know. No matter how much money you sink into the most modern and expensive electronics, they don't exactly know how to run themselves."

Hackworth crossed his arms and stared to the side, toward Mark's feet.

"I'm about to be more honest than I want to, Bill. Right now is not the time."

McConvey threw his hands up and barked out a harsh laugh that echoed against the stone and coal walls.

"Not the time to be honest? Come on now, man. We got a situation here none of us can figure out, and a first-rate expert who might be able to help our poor ignorant selves for a change instead of scolding us and slapping us on the wrist. When do you think you'll get around to your anticipated honesty breakthrough?"

Mark ignored the pointless jab like he always did. He'd heard much worse in far less challenging circumstances.

Hackworth stood still, but he shook his head.

"My sensors are just fine, Bill, and you know it. I'm not going to stand here and be scolded like a damn kid. I've been talking to you about strange trouble in this area for a long time now, and you deny knowing anything about it. We're way past worrying about a couple of fines for water if the damn mine is shaking and we can't figure out why."

"Stop and look around you, water bug," Papaw said, faint and distant, but the words were clear.

Mark had wandered far enough away that the men didn't seem to be paying attention to him any more. He watched Grissom join the other two out of the corner of his eye while he leaned closer to the rock face.

The dry, evenly white rock face that hadn't been wetted down any time in the recent past.

And yet beads and trickles of water glistened in several spots.

"What the hell are you talking about, Hackworth?" Grissom stood with hands on hips, voice as loud as Mark had ever heard it.

"I'm talking about the way my miners hear noises where they shouldn't. Not enough to set off the sensors, but more creaks and groans than a room no one's worked for a year could account for. Almost like someone else *is* working it on the other side."

"What's happening there, Papaw?" Mark whispered.

"Starting to get riled up again. Can't tell if your side or mine is stirring up the other. Could be it's both. I sure would feel a lot better if you got yourself away from there."

Mark walked back toward the group, watching McConvey loom over Hackworth, who stared back defiant.

"Please correct me if I'm wrong," McConvey said. "And I *must* be wrong. Because I'm sure I didn't just hear you accuse me of running an unpermitted and unplanned operation."

Hackworth held his arms out wide, shaking his head.

"You tell me, Bill. You decide to open a new chamber without letting anyone know? Without any kind of safety review? Or maybe you just wanted somewhere to dump your tailings and wastewater. To hell with anyone who might be operating or trying to live nearby."

McConvey stood almost toe-to-toe with Hackworth, leaning forward until their masks were inches apart.

"I'll take every last damn one of you over there right now!" McConvey shouted. "Have Mr. Hersch call in a bunch of his regulation-happy buddies from Big Stone Gap and Richmond, and we'll go over it all with a ruler and a fine-toothed comb. You've lost what little brain you have in your empty head if you think you can pin your troubles on me!"

"Then what do you expect me to believe is going on down here?" Hackworth said. He rounded on Mark, fists clenched at his sides. "I'm going to take a guess you found what you were looking for. Right?"

Mark looked from one to the other of them, judging the lay of the emotional land.

Hackworth red-faced and angry, McConvey stone-faced and furious. Grissom watching them both, his own features as carefully neutral as if he were watching paint dry.

"What I found is water where it shouldn't be," Mark said, deliberately calm. "Not much, mind you, but enough to get my attention on an otherwise dry wall. What should I be looking for instead, Mr. Hackworth?"

CHAPTER 14

BETH TURNED off the engine in Mark's car, trying not to think too much about where he was right now.

Instead, she focused on being in the same space he usually was in so many ways. The same seat he spent countless hours in, often on the way to see her over the months before he moved back home to Bountyfield.

They were so close to the same height that she hadn't adjusted the seat or the mirrors or anything else. The steering wheel was only a tiny bit lower than the one in her car.

It was no wonder they constantly traded his old t-shirt back and forth.

She turned to Lisa Harrison in the seat beside her, her anxious mind wondering for a brief second about all the possible car seat adjustments Lisa and Susan required with several inches in height between them.

"We were a little bit further along the creek than you got today," Beth said. "When Mark did the demonstration."

"All right. Let's get out there and see if we can help him."

The night air had taken on a soft humidity the day didn't have, playing up the scent of pine trees. All the water in the atmosphere transformed the faint orange light from the mine to a glowing nimbus outlining the high ridge in front of them.

They walked in companionable silence, Beth again focusing on the trail and Lisa shining her light on the stream itself.

The grass had mostly rebounded from the group of people who walked out that morning, with only the remnants of gravel dust showing where they'd passed. The footprints she and Mark made were still flattened, and clearly visible as the only spaces that didn't reflect the gathering dew.

"Stop me if I'm being nosy," Lisa said, "but did you two have a reason to come back out here earlier? I'm all for spending private time together in the great outdoors, but Isom Gap has plenty of better places for that."

Beth did her level best to keep a laugh from escaping, but a soft snort made it through after all.

It was an entirely fair question, but how on earth to answer it honestly without sounding crazy?

"Mark is doing just fine right now," Papaw said. "I got a strong feeling you can talk to her. Her people standing right here with us feel the same way."

Beth took a deep breath and decided to trust the man Mark trusted so much. And wish for the thousandth time that she'd met him.

"Let me ask you a weird question," she said. "What would you say if I asked if you've ever seen a ghost?"

Lisa didn't break stride, but she did take a good long look at Beth.

"Well, I'd say I've never seen one that I knew what I was seeing." She paused for several of her long steps. "It's possible I missed all the signs that were right in front of my eyes, of course. But I'd also say I'm convinced I've *felt* one a time or two. Or smelled them."

"You're not going to make me ask you to tell me what that means, are you?"

Lisa laughed and shook her head.

"Any number of my relatives dead or alive would smack me a good one if I was that rude. Nothing all that dramatic, not like moving furniture or my keys disappearing from one place and showing up somewhere else. There have been a few times where I got that prickly feeling up and down my spine, to start with."

She glanced at Beth before she went on.

"The main thing I can point to is a smell where it couldn't be. A few times I smelled my Granny's perfume years after she was gone. Or my Uncle Si's buttermilk biscuits like they were fresh out of the oven. I was at home by myself both times. Once or twice, I was sure I'd walked right into the middle of the biggest spiderweb that ever was. When not only was there nothing at all in my path, but I was so far underground that no spider could have possibly been there."

"Did anything happen after that? When you felt the spiderweb?"

Lisa shrugged. "Yeah, things no one besides Susan knows about. One time there was a rock fall in that spot I backed out of only a few minutes before. Then another time, turned out a big power cable I was about to step over had a flaw in it. I called in an electrician to check it, saved myself or someone else a pretty bad shock. Might have saved my life that day."

Beth slowed as the end of the footprints in the dew came into sight.

"Thank you for telling me, Lisa. I won't say a word to anyone else. For now, all I'll say is we came out here this afternoon to chase a few spiderwebs of our own. Maybe we can trade ghost stories when things calm down."

Lisa stepped over to the edge of the stream, where the yellow streak still showed in the water.

"No mistaking that smell," she said. "Look about the same as when you two left here?"

"It does. Smells about the same too."

Lisa nodded, then played her light around the darker footprints in the grass. Right over to the rock where Mark and Beth sat to wait for the ghosts to figure out what was happening on their side.

"Got you another good'un there," Clina said. "I can tell you right now her people are the only ones besides Jacob Stanley who see fit to talk to us, and to want to help the ones still on your side of the veil."

Lisa touched the rock with the toe of her black leather boot.

"I have no doubt you're not the kind who likes to dance around what needs to be said or done. So I'll just ask. Want to tell me more about what happened out here now? Looks to me like you two got comfortable for at least a little while."

Beth hesitated, pretending to examine the boulder's surface, and aware she was fooling exactly no one. She covered her mouth with one hand and spoke under her breath.

"Warn me if anything seems to be going wrong here? And if something happens with Mark?"

"You know we will," Papaw whispered.

She turned and looked Lisa in the eye by the light of their two flashlights.

"Part of it was after Mark let Mr. McConvey know what was going on, he wanted to keep an eye on the creek. But we were following one of those spiderwebs for sure. If we hadn't been doing that, we would have missed the shake altogether, and the runoff breaking through."

Beth scrubbed her face, having a furious debate with

herself over how much to admit. Telling Lisa that a long-dead boy trying to get through to Mark might have *caused* the shake was very much a step too far.

The need for help, and worry over where he was right now, pushed her over to speaking up as much as she could.

"Something's wrong out here, Lisa. Something that may have been wrong for a long time. Hell, it may be part of that old trouble from years and years back that Susan told me about today."

Lisa nodded slowly.

"What's Mark looking for under the ground right now, Beth? What do you think we can do about it from up here?"

"If my impression of you is right, you know the mine maps every bit as well as Mark does. Can you think of anywhere this kind of runoff should be coming from? It's been running foul like this for what, almost an hour now?"

"An hour sounds about right if you two saw it start up. Mark strikes me as the kind who has the whole mountain and everything underneath it memorized. I'm not quite as focused on the other operations as he is, but yeah, I'm familiar. McConvey is the local emergency coordinator, and he's damn good at it. I'm the search and rescue coordinator, so I'm no slouch myself. I can't think of a thing in the world that makes sense."

The radio blipped, and Lisa raised it immediately and tapped something to make it blip again. A man spoke in clipped words.

"They're at the rock face. No trouble. Investigating now. Over."

"Understood. Standing by."

Beth held one hand over her heart, not wanting to admit how hard it pounded now. Lisa half-smiled.

"He's still fine, Beth. Strange happenings tonight, sure, but the mines right here are remarkably stable. Grissom might seem about as lifeless and dull as Hackworth is obnoxious. Hell, Hackworth is as irritating as a teenage boy loaded up on sugar and caffeine once he gets to showing off, and a loudmouth on top of that. But they both run a good outfit."

"Mark says pretty much the same thing. That's why I'm confused about where the water could be coming from. Sounds like you know a good bit about water. What do you think?"

Lisa pointed her light straight up, then traced the tops of the trees with it.

"I don't like the idea of this," she said slowly. "But it could be illegally stored sludge and wastewater from somewhere else. Trying to hide it instead of dealing with it. That wouldn't likely be anyone but Grissom or Hackworth from where we're standing. I doubt anyone else could get access."

She waved one hand up the creek.

"Not unless it's McConvey, and the whole thing is further up than here. Hell, any one of them could have worked into a section they're not supposed to. But that flat doesn't make sense with what I know of them. Now, what did you mean about the old feud around here? How does that tie in?"

"I'm not sure it does. Did Susan tell you about that photo someone brought in today?"

Lisa grinned. "You mean Deborah Fleming? That poor woman has had a hard way to go pretty much her whole life, but she always means well. I can tell you Suze was tickled to death with that photo. Just about scampered back to her huge monitor the second she walked in the door. Zoomed in until I swear I could count the hairs in every man's nostrils."

Beth smiled, remembering how she'd zoomed in on the glass plate images of Clina, and on the tombstones around her for names to check out at the Boun County courthouse.

"Susan was sure she'd be able to get all the missing names

worked out," Beth said. "I figure she'll have most of them by the time I see her tomorrow."

"I can damn well guarantee she will. She had a bunch of them done by the time I got the call to head back out here. Her dad gave her a bunch of old books and photos and stuff that he helped carry out of that old house the state uses now. Where we met Mark this morning. The folks who lived there got a little bit...overly attached to Isom Gap history. Pretty much had their own library in there, but not much room for anything else."

Beth froze, all at once verging on desperate to know what Susan had discovered.

"She mentioned that today. Said the historical society wasn't interested?"

Lisa snorted and pointed her light at the water again before moving it back to the boulder.

"Yeah, her dad told us all about that. Called them the hysterical society after they turned him down without even looking at what he had. I'd bet they'll change their tune after her stuff helped with that photo today."

"Do you remember any of the names?" Beth said, trying not to hold her breath.

"Sure, that's what caught my attention. Susan found two boys named McConvey and Grissom that looked about the same age as Jacob Stanley, and matched up the Hackworth already marked on the back for sure. All on that same crew as Jacob when he got killed. I know just about everyone in Isom Gap has family that's been here since the dawn of time, or they claim to. Still, that struck me as kind of a strange coincidence, you know?"

Beth swallowed, trying to keep her imagination from running away with her. She sank down to the cold boulder and turned her head to the side.

"Could that be right?" she whispered, too quiet for even

herself to hear. "And that's where the dead spot and even the bad water is coming from? Ancestors of the same people who are underground with Mark right now were part of that original feud?"

"Afraid that probably is the truth," Clina said as a chorus of shouts rang out on her side. "Jacob Stanley just lit out after a couple of boys running like the wind, right toward that dead spot in the world."

CHAPTER 15

THE CHARGED silence in the mine chamber combined with the swirling discussions Mark could barely hear from the ghostly side to make his head throb. But he didn't dare step in and try to reduce the tension.

He needed to know what Hackworth was talking about too badly for that.

Water where it shouldn't be was always a concern, especially inside a mine. Mark had learned that lesson the hard way as a kid, in a dirt basement with flooding no one could see or know about until he was literally in the middle of it.

But if Hackworth was talking about something else instead—maybe accusing McConvey or even Grissom of breaking the law—answering Mark's question about what the problem might be mattered even more

At least until he heard young men shouting, followed immediately by Papaw's voice.

"You want to take care, Mark. Jacob just now went charging off after two other boys. Likely got a lot more to do with what's going on under that mountain than we knew."

Hackworth turned and strode past Mark, going unerringly to the spot with water seeping through.

"I'm willing to bet you found the seep without a bit of trouble, Mr. Hersch. You know better than I do that water doesn't just appear where it hasn't been for years. Not unless something changed to let it get there. What we've all got to know is what *did* change? And who changed it?"

"I think we all need to calm down, Hackworth," Grissom said, walking toward the wall himself. "Yelling at each other won't solve a damn thing, but it might well distract us enough to miss the real trouble. Kind of trouble that might get us killed."

"*Killed*, Grissom?" McConvey said, hands again on his hips. "Don't you think you're picking up Hackworth's unfortunate habit of exaggeration yourself now?"

"No, Bill, I do *not* think I'm exaggerating," Grissom said. "Something shook the ground within the hour. Now we've got runoff from an unexplained source, and I can see the water seeping through right here with my own eyes. Same as Hackworth, and Mr. Hersch here. It's curious how you're the only one who can't see we have to take some kind of action."

"I see it just fine," McConvey said. "Where I'm struggling is trying to work that tiny bit of water up into some kind of dire emergency."

Mark focused on McConvey at the same time Clina and his Papaw whispered for him to watch out.

Had he misjudged McConvey after several years of working with him?

Was the uproar among the ghosts turning these men against each other, or the other way around?

Or were Mark's own nerves overstretched enough to have him turning into the paranoid one himself?

"Hang on and listen," he said. "This face is close to the stream's path, so there could be groundwater. That alone would be a change that makes me uncomfortable at best. A flooded chamber is another possibility I can't dismiss without knowing more. That could put all of us at risk, and anyone else who comes into this mine. I have to ask both of you— no, all three of you. Do you know about anything on the other side of this wall that I need to be concerned about?"

Hackworth shook his head without hesitation, then stepped closer to Mark. Almost as if he expected some sort of protection Mark was neither willing nor able to give.

"I don't give a damn what they think," Hackworth said. "Or what they do or don't want me to say. This face acts like something is going on over on the other side. Enough that I don't much like to be standing right here, but I'm not going to back off on this until I know the truth."

Mark bit the inside of his cheek and absolutely forbade himself to giggle. If Hackworth had any idea how close he was to the reality of the thing in worrying about trouble on the other side, this conversation would go a very different way.

Increased shouting on that other side warned him before his Papaw spoke.

"I don't quite know what happened out of sight, but I see Jacob Stanley coming back this way. Him and a man that wasn't here before brought those boys that ran off with them. I'd imagine both boys with their arms twisted right up against their backs started the fussing."

"Can you tell me their names, Papaw?"

"Here now! No call to shove them right up in my face, Jacob. Best tell me who they are first thing."

After a pause, Mark had his answers, and a hell of a lot more questions.

If the connection between the ghost world and their own held true, he and Hackworth did indeed stand on the opposite side from McConvey and Grissom.

The long-lost spirit of Purvis Lee Hackworth had even found his way back to stand with Jacob Stanley. One of them holding tight to a spitting-mad Eural Joe McConvey, the other to an equally furious Carlis Grissom.

And down in the depths of this coal mine with an unknown water hazard, only Mark knew the mountain itself got agitated by angry humans *and* angry ghosts.

He had to figure out what that meant, and what he could do about it.

"Okay then," he said. "I'm concerned enough about this to call in a crew for a full investigation. We'll be going behind this wall one way or the other. You'll all have to ask yourselves whether you want to be standing right here when they break through, or whether we'll come at it from a different approach."

All three of these men were smart and experienced enough to know Mark was exaggerating at least a bit. He was counting on them seeing the reality of the risk they were pushing themselves and everyone else into.

Hackworth glanced at him for a quick second before standing up straight and regaining a little of his smart-ass swagger.

"You've got my permission right this second, Mr. Hersch. I'll even approve the loan of any of my *expensive*, modern equipment you might need. I don't have a thing in the world to hide. I'm sure my fellow operators here will accept my invitation to stand right here and observe. Just to make certain precautions are taken for everybody's safety, and everything is on the level, you understand."

"Count me in on that," Grissom said, louder than Mark had ever heard him speak. "You got the run of my operation, too, and anyone else you need to bring with you. Guess we'll see if McConvey here comes up with a reason to decline."

"Grab onto him!" Papaw shouted. "That McConvey boy

just about took the Grissom boy's head plum off. Others jumped right into the brawl."

McConvey stepped toward Grissom, raising his hand in what Mark hoped was a rude gesture rather than a clenched fist.

Before he got a word out, Papaw cried "Look out, Mark!"

A split-second later the ground and walls rumbled around them.

Mark spun away and crouched as the trickle of water in front of him burst out in a freezing cold jet.

CHAPTER 16

BETH SHOT to her feet as the ground shook under her again.

If anything harder than before.

Lisa raised the radio before the tremor faded away.

"Status report! What's going on there?"

Only a couple of seconds passed before the answer, but Beth's heart pounded too many times to count. The furious shouting and scuffle in Clina's world was far louder as well, and the too-familiar names of the fighters chased themselves viciously in her mind.

Beth struggled not to let her heart fall into a swirling black pit of rock and dust and fire and water. All of it close enough for shouting if Mark was aboveground where he was *supposed* to be.

Instead endless tons of mountain separated them, as it might do forever.

A surprisingly clear voice spoke over the radio.

"Got alarms for that shake, but nothing for ignition or roof falls. Repeat, no indication of ignition or roof fall. Awaiting response from the driver."

Lisa scowled and shook her head. "No word at all? Try him again, *now*."

Beth grabbed Lisa's arm without thinking, trying to drag her mind through all the crowd noise to something rational in her own world.

"Mark thinks there's water there, maybe a flooded chamber. Would an alarm sound if that broke through?"

Instead of answering, Lisa jerked hard enough to drop the radio. She bent to pick it up and stood slowly, staring hard at Beth.

"There would be a flood alert, yes. If the water hits the sensor. If any of that happened at... What the hell *was* that, Beth? All that shouting and noise?"

Beth held her hand against her chest, not sure which direction her terrified heart and mind would dart toward next.

"You...you heard that? Most people... Why wouldn't the driver answer?"

Lisa held up the radio, still staring. The red and green lights blinked away.

"If he dropped his radio like my dumb ass just did, it would have landed on solid rock or maybe into water instead of a bunch of weeds. Might take a minute to get to the emergency box depending on where they are. Now listen to me, what *was* that?"

"That was... I have no idea how to tell you. Can't someone else get down there to see what's wrong?"

The radio blipped.

"Got a second crew on the way to the—" A higher blip cut in. "Stand by, this should be them."

"Someone else will get there as fast as they can," Lisa said. "Don't tell me then. *Show* me."

She tucked the radio against her ribs and held out her arm.

Beth couldn't think of anything else to say or do. She gripped Lisa's forearm just as Clina spoke up loud and clear.

"Your feller is fine, Beth. Startled and shook up is all. Got a right good soaking. You heard the dust up with all those boys over here. We figure that caused the dead spot to rattle on both sides. Might have caused tempers to rattle on your side from the way it sounded."

Clutching her charm through Mark's t-shirt, Beth tried to smile at Lisa through her tears just as the radio blipped again.

"All good underground. Had a water breach, nothing severe. Enough to make a mess. The driver's radio was damaged, that was the delay. They'll get headed back up top soon as they finish their investigation."

Lisa slowly raised her radio.

"Understood. We'll verify with… We'll check conditions here and head back ourselves."

She turned her flashlight toward the creek, but Beth didn't need to see to know the runoff was worse.

She smelled it.

Sure enough, the streak of discolored water was wider, and shaded from yellow to orange.

"Want to tell me what was I hearing there?" Lisa said. "And what *both sides* did something rattle on? Did that woman say a *dead* spot?"

Beth laughed and immediately let go of Lisa's arm.

"I'm sorry, Lisa, I'm not laughing at you. I'm more relieved than anything. I thought… Never mind what I thought. You're only the third person I know of besides me who *can* hear them. I guess you could say you're hearing my spiderwebs. Or maybe my spiders."

Lisa raised her eyebrows, but she looked more curious than confused.

"The ground shook there too? Wherever they are? Where the hell *are* they, and exactly who are we talking about?"

Beth shook her head, but she couldn't stop smiling.

Turned out even a few seconds of believing her deepest fear had come true and then getting a reprieve did that to her.

Mark was okay.

She very much needed to get a good hold of him and verify that for herself, but having the opportunity to *do* that was everything.

"I'll try to explain as we go. They're here, or what here was. Two of them came with me. With us. My friend Clina and Mark's grandfather. His Papaw. I know I'm not making any sense, I'm sorry. Give me a minute to get myself back together."

Lisa took a deep breath and pointed the light back at the creek for a second. Then she slipped the radio into her jacket pocket and they started walking back toward the car.

"I don't want to drop the damn thing again. Are you trying to tell me you brought ghosts here with you? And they're what, talking to our local ghosts now? Setting up some kind of spectral gossip network?"

"Got someone here who might be able to help," Papaw said. "Says Lisa will remember her and no doubt about it."

"Mark's Papaw has someone who wants to talk to you," Beth said. "Right there with him. Someone you're sure to remember."

CHAPTER 17

MARK SLOWLY LOWERED HIS FREEZING, soaking wet hands from the back of his head, not quite sure how much water had just gushed over and seemingly right through him. Even his hair under the hardhat was dripping, and his toes squished inside his boots when he shifted.

He was still upright, more or less. On his knees, yeah, but the force hadn't been enough to tumble him sideways or forward.

His pounding heart and laboring lungs hadn't accepted the reality of the near miss just yet. The fact that his Papaw spoke inside his head rather than standing right beside him brought him a long way toward realizing which side of the world he was on.

"Mark? I got a feeling you're still doing okay, but I sure would like to hear that from you."

"I'm okay," Mark said, managing to keep his voice under the noise of his respiration. "Wet and cold, but still breathing."

"Good. These knuckleheads and their damn foolishness broke that dead spot open right down the middle, but didn't get a thing to show for it. I'm watching it shrink away right this second."

"Sounds a lot like what happened here."

Mark blinked several times through his wavering, foggy vision before he realized his safety glasses were the problem. He pulled them off and braved a look around.

Hackworth had hit the rock floor quite a bit harder from the way he slowly moved around into a sitting position. A smeary mix of white and black dust coated his face, mask, and coveralls, and his hardhat had disappeared.

A much less drenched Grissom squatted beside Hackworth about the same time McConvey grabbed Mark's shoulders.

"Hersch? You okay? Mark? You didn't get a lungful, did you?"

Mark shook his head, raising one hand to point to his respirator, still firmly in place. Catching his breath while wearing it wasn't his favorite activity, but trying to cough up water full of coal dust and heavy metals and who knew what else out of his chest would have been about a thousand times worse.

"Not a drop, not in my lungs anyway. The rest of me took up all the slack."

McConvey's broad shoulders slumped and his head dropped forward for a second.

"When I saw all that water, I thought you were done for. Hell, I thought we were *all* done for when it broke loose. Can you stand? Everything in the right place?"

Mark nodded and gladly let McConvey pull him up, only then noticing how much his knees hurt from hitting solid stone. Skipping the simple precaution of wearing kneepads didn't seem like the best decision he'd ever made, even though they had no expectation of crawling through narrow passages when they suited up.

He'd have nasty bruises to deal with over the next few days.

Buried in that thought was the spectacular reality that he'd get to *have* a next few days.

He hadn't been so sure about that when the water hit him.

"What happened?" he said. "Everyone else okay?"

McConvey held Mark's arm until he was steady, then waved toward the rock face.

"Damn wall went a-gusher. Not as bad as it could have been, of course. It was over in a few seconds. I saw you turn and drop, then it bowled Hackworth over. By the time I could run over here, it was all played out."

He paused and waved in the other direction, toward the mantrip and the main corridor.

"Driver ran toward us, dropped his radio halfway. He's fine, but I guess that radio is down for the count."

Alarm jetted through Mark harder than the water had.

"Does the surface know? That we're okay, I mean? We *have* to get word to them after a shake like that."

McConvey grabbed Mark's shoulder again, but this time it was more reassuring than alarming.

"He got to the main box on the wall. They know we're all right, Mark. *She* knows."

Mark nodded, doing his best to ignore the unpleasantly cold water still managing to trickle down his chest and back. For all the protection his coveralls offered against the ever-present dust, they seemed to only make the aftereffects of a dousing that much worse.

His Papaw spoke up, offering more calm than McConvey or anyone else on this side of the veil besides Beth could have.

"I let her know right away, water bug. Me and Clina both. We got all these squalling boys spread out apart now, so

I expect everything will be fine where you are. I'm sure I don't have to remind you I was right close by when you got a surprise soaking once upon a time. This time was actually a hell of a lot less scary. At least for me."

An unexpected fall into a flooded shaft when Mark was just a kid had served as his introduction to the horrors of swallowing properly fouled water.

"I remember," Mark whispered. "But I have to say this time was worse for me. You could reach out and grab me then, and save my scrawny teenaged backside. If you'd grabbed me just now, I would have been on the wrong side of the veil for sure."

He turned back toward the wall, grateful when McConvey put a working flashlight into his hand.

The white rock dust was gone in a jagged streak, leaving black coal and gray stone underneath. Water still trickled out along a crack about two feet long. The breach in the rock face was barely wide enough to fit the tips of his fingers into, but it had been plenty big enough to let a torrent through.

The rupture was nowhere near as bad as it could have been, thank the gods of geology and gravity. He had to give more credit to unruly ghosts for letting it loose before it built up even worse than he was comfortable admitting until he got back aboveground.

"I think we can safely say there was a flooded chamber," Mark said, unable to keep the amusement out of his voice now that he'd finally caught his breath. "Probably best to get this wall opened up and see what's going on before it starts to fill again, if it does."

Hackworth and Grissom walked over to join them at the wall, both of them more or less steady on their feet. Hackworth had retrieved his hardhat and at least smudged the grime on his face around pretty good.

"I'm on board with that," he said. "See if we can all figure out how to stop this from happening again."

Grissom reached out to touch the new crack much like Mark had.

"I'm not picking up a trace of sulfur stink, and that water didn't look yellow to me. The change in the water table that let this build up might be part of the same thing that's causing the runoff out in the creek. But I don't think it *came* from here."

Mark shook his head, not about to say the truth he knew in his bones.

The ghostly residents of Isom Gap might not have created the somehow-linked dead spot and newly flooded chamber. But the ornery participants in the long-ago feud were certainly having an effect on the weakness in the veil, one that linked up in a dangerous way with the living.

He couldn't imagine trying to explain one bit of that to these descendants of the feud, who were finally on the same side in looking to solve the problem.

He doubted he'd ever talk to much of anyone in the whole world besides Beth about such things.

He closed his eyes at the thought of her.

Once what now felt like an endless conversation finally finished up, he'd get to return to the surface of the earth rather than drowning in freezing blackness.

Breathe fresh air, look at the stars.

See the sun come up in the morning, but not until after he took a long, scalding hot bath tonight.

Hold Beth in his arms as soon as humanly possible, longer if he could convince her to let him.

McConvey dragged him back into his cold, damp reality.

"I hope we'll all pitch in and get it worked out. With your help of course, Mr. Hersch." He looked down, kicking the toe of one booted foot into a grayish puddle, exactly like a chagrined little boy. "I owe you an apology, Hackworth. I decided you were full of shit earlier for no reason other than thinking you were accusing me of causing all this trouble."

"Yeah, I need to get in on that myself," Grissom said, concentrating on brushing at his barely wet and dirty coveralls. "Had that nonsense in my empty head, too. I'm sorry about that, and that goes to both of you."

Hackworth stared at them for a few seconds, water and muck coating his face and neck, before he burst out into his typical loud guffaws.

"Aw hell, boys. I sure do appreciate you, and I'm real sorry myself about all this foolishness. Especially since I *did* think you were storing up some kind of record-breaking load of toxic waste right here under my nose. Enough to bring Mr. Hersch here charging in on a white horse and raining down a regular blizzard of violations."

Mark joined in the laughter for a few seconds, until a shiver hard enough to rattle his teeth took hold of him.

"I'm flattered by the imagery, gentlemen. And I'm about to freeze to death standing here. Time for me to get out of this mine for the night and leave the cleanup to you."

Another back-pounding round of laughter ensued, but that did get everyone heading across the wet and puddled ground toward the mantrip. The driver—boots and pants wet all the way up to the knees—swung himself down into the seat, obviously ready to go.

Hackworth showed more evidence of recovering his normal rather exuberant personality before they made it halfway when he elbowed Mark with a huge grin.

"Got a good idea of how you want to get warmed up, do you? Something to do with our special lunch guest this afternoon?"

Mark nodded and tipped his hardhat, smiling in return.

"Absolutely right, Mr. Hackworth. I only hope the rest of you are half as lucky as me."

CHAPTER 18

LISA SCOWLED and shook her head at Beth's offer of someone needing to talk to her from Clina's side, but she slowed her pace.

Beth was determined to wait and let her come to understanding the spirit world all around them in her own time and way.

The excited chatter gradually taking over from the roiling sounds of anger inside her mind gave her hope that Lisa would do just that. Along with an unknown person who'd passed over, waiting to reconnect across the void of death.

Lisa finally stopped, turning to face Beth with her arms crossed. Right beside the dusty spot where Mark and the other operators met that morning, what felt like a lifetime ago.

"I don't mean to be harsh with you, Beth, but this sounds like some kind of twisted Appalachian hillbilly version of a Ouija board."

Beth let that stand for a few beats of her heart before answering.

"I know how strange it sounds. Believe me. I was terrified

to tell Mark, and that only a week after we first met. It never occurred to me that you would be able to hear them too, same way he does."

"So Mark hears them, huh? That man is a real sweetheart once you pay attention past him being tough as nails and smart as hell. *And* he's about as far from being into silly fringe beliefs and fanciful bullshit as anyone I've ever met. No offense to you, but I did only meet you today. I have to say the fact that he's so obviously a goner when it comes to you speaks volumes for your character."

Beth didn't care one bit if her blush showed.

"No offense taken. I would have laughed you right off this mountain if you'd suggested such a thing to me a year ago. But it's true. Mark *does* hear them. We just figured out tonight how he can hear his grandfather even when he's away from me."

Beth held out her hand, and after a few seconds hesitation, Lisa gripped it hard. Her fingers were rough and cold.

"Okay," Beth said. "Lisa can hear you now."

"Hey there Lisa Lisa," a woman's voice said, nowhere near as old as Clina or Papaw. "Bet you never thought you'd have to deal with my annoying ass again."

Lisa's hard, doubtful features softened, and she let out a gasping sob.

"*Erin*? I don't... How is this possible? Is it really you?"

"Afraid so, big sister. Let me see, how can I convince you? When we were kids, sometimes if I begged hard enough, you'd let me sneak into your bed if I had a bad dream. I then proceeded to twist my fingers through your hair so I could feel safe and get back to sleep. Took you ages to get the tangles out, but you still let me do it."

Lisa laughed and choked back tears.

"You've been here this whole time? Right here?"

"Well, I think it took me a while to find my way to

where I am. Might not have recognized it at all if I hadn't run into a couple of people I know. It's Isom Gap, but from a long time before we were born. They say this version moves forward in time at about a snail's pace, so we'll see what happens."

"Someone else is there?" Lisa said. Her grip loosened on Beth's hand, but she showed no signs of letting go. "I mean, I heard a bunch of people earlier, but there's someone else I know?"

"I'd like to think my niece remembers her favorite uncle," a man's deep voice said, again sounding far younger than the ghosts Beth was used to hearing.

This time Lisa put the flashlight into her pocket without even turning it off and covered her heart. She kept right on smiling, and she laughed again before she wiped her tears.

"Uncle Si? I might have known you were too stubborn to fade away into nothing like a sensible person. Is the whole family there? Everyone from Isom Gap?"

"No, honey," Uncle Si said. "A whole lot of them, sure. But not everyone seems to find their way here. Erin did take a few years as far as I can tell, 'cause she got here after I did. I'm awful glad she made it."

Lisa shook her head and blinked several times.

"I've got about a hundred thousand questions for both of you, and any other ghosts that might be hanging around. But we're having trouble here that I'm scared half to death about getting worse. Can anybody tell me what's going on with the ground shaking here? Or that dead spot I heard one of you talk about?"

Beth heard both Erin and Uncle Si laugh.

"Haven't changed at all," Erin said. "Still my pain-in-the-ass big sister. Right to the point and straight on 'til the problem's solved. It seems to me that a weak spot that's been here for a long, long time started getting worse over the last little bit. Keeping up with time is tricky, but I did see it change. Something was about to break through, from what I can tell."

"Now it looks like the whole thing about drained away," Uncle Si said. "From what I'm hearing your people say, Beth, sounds like that big dust-up we had here cracked the whole thing a good one on both sides. Just about down to a crooked streak on the ground now."

"The dead spot I keep hearing about," Beth said. "That's one reason Mark wanted to go underground. To see if that was tied up with the trouble with the water here."

"And then the ground shook and something *did* break through," Lisa said, shaking her head, but she was smiling. "Drained away here, too. Listen, how did Mark manage to hear without being with you, Beth? I doubt very much that you'll want to stay right here beside me long enough for all the talking I want to do."

Beth got disturbingly close to a giggle this time.

"He gave me his grandmother's engagement ring a few weeks ago. As a placeholder, which he makes very sure to tell me, and often. I have a necklace that came from… Never mind, I'll tell you all about that later. When he put the ring on, he could hear his grandfather. So maybe if you have something that had a strong connection with your sister or your uncle?"

Lisa squeezed Beth's hand with both of hers.

"I think I have the very thing. Maybe you and Mark can come over to the house, maybe tomorrow for dinner, and we can try it. But I guess we really should get over there and see what happened at the mine."

"Sure thing," Uncle Si said, and Erin chimed in a second later. "Now that we know we can, we'll talk you ear off for sure."

Lisa lowered her head for a second, then let go of Beth's hand.

"Thank you. Thank you so, so much. Erin passed away when she was fourteen and I was seventeen. And Uncle Simon left us a few years later. You have no idea what this means to me."

"I haven't met any of my people yet, but I know how much it means for Mark to talk to his Papaw again. That first day when I heard Clina, I thought I was losing my mind. I never imagined I'd be able to help people on this side of the veil, but I'm so glad I can."

Lisa darted forward and hugged Beth hard enough to squeeze her breath away. Then she got her flashlight back out and squared her shoulders.

"Now, let's get back over to Hackworth's operation and see if we can't straighten out their mess before all these men manage to make it even worse."

CHAPTER 19

MARK DID his level best not to push against the metal grate door of the huge freight elevator on the way up. No need to give the men around him any more reason to carry on about Beth.

But he wouldn't have hesitated to move one of them out of the way if they tried to stand in front of him. He got the feeling they understood that, teasing or not.

Not one of them even pretended to step forward when the elevator jolted to a stop.

Cool as the October nighttime air was, it felt warm compared to the depths of the mine. The simple lack of gigantic fans blowing at all times made a huge difference on its own.

He never thought he'd welcome the thick smell of diesel fumes invading his nostrils. Or the noise of a chattering crowd just waiting to serve as an audience he very much did not want.

The glare of floodlights kept him from seeing out into the crowd for what felt like an hour of watching the door creep and crawl itself up out of the way. Mark ducked under and got several feet out onto the gravels before it quite managed the job.

Only a streak of motion warned him before Beth collided with him hard enough to knock him back a step. He dropped the hardhat and respirator without a second's thought so he could hold on tight.

"Gods, you're *freezing*," she said, her lips sending a blast of warmth from his ear through his entire body.

"Not anymore," he whispered. "Right now everything is perfect."

She drew back enough to look into his eyes and brush back his damp and entirely unmanageable hair.

"I think we can do better, don't you?" She kissed him and warmed the rest of him up nicely.

"We will do better, soon as I get myself cleaned up. That's a promise."

Beth laughed and leaned forward to hold her smooth cheek against his now scruffy one.

"I'll help you get cleaned up, don't you worry. Our cabin has a bathtub big enough for two."

Mark finally looked around, expecting the gathering of rugged locals to be waiting for their chance for a good bout of teasing. But the whole group had already moved to right outside the machine shop, and McConvey, Grissom, and Hackworth were pulling off their coveralls and accepting steaming cups of what had to be industrial strength coffee.

"Think they'll let us sneak away?" he said, nodding in that direction.

"I think they might. But then you'd never hear the end of it, would you?"

"I probably won't already, not that I give a damn about that. I guess it would make sense to leave these filthy coveralls here instead of mucking up the car worse than I have to."

A quick search for his abandoned hat and respirator turned up nothing until he realized one of the others must have grabbed them on the way out. More fodder for the teasing mill that he would gladly put up with now that Beth was by his side.

By the time they made it to the machine shop, McConvey, Grissom, and Hackworth were back down to their street clothes and huddled together with Lisa Harrison. With any luck, getting themselves to a quick agreement about how to handle the next few days.

"How did you and Hackworth end up getting the worst of it?" Beth said, helping Mark balance on one foot to pull the sopping wet legs of the coveralls off. "I think you have even him beat."

Hackworth was indeed the only other one whose jeans and shirt were wet through, at least down his front side. He'd brushed his brown hair straight back into an unflattering but more-or-less orderly mop.

Mark's troublesome hair, on the other hand, was responding in the usual way to an unexpected and uncontrolled soak. Meaning twisting itself into all manner of ill-behaved snarls and tangles.

"We were the only ones standing beside the rock face when it let go," he said. "That reminds me, I'd like to speak to someone on the other side about that. A warning would have been nice."

The contact with Beth and wearing his grandmother's ring seemed to amplify Mark's access to the ghost world, so he quite clearly heard more laughter than Clina and his Papaw could account for.

"You know I would have shouted out sooner if I could have, water bug," Papaw said. "Things got pretty ornery around here just then. Young Jacob Stanley will want to talk to you, Mark. To thank you. None of us ever can yet figure out why, but the way he locked onto you kept a dangerous thing from getting even worse."

"That sounds fine to me," Mark said. "I'm glad I could help for whatever reason. Hopefully things will settle down there like I think they will here now that the pressure's off."

"Can't say it's like to ever be close to a normal town," Clina said. "But I reckon anything is a step toward the better after years of keeping themselves so stirred up."

Mark stepped away to add his coveralls to the filthy pile, and finally got a good look at Beth when he turned back. Her clothes and hands, even her face were smudged with the same mix of rock dust and coal dust he'd be scrubbing off of himself.

"I'm sorry, sweetheart. You're almost as dirty as me."

Beth kissed his cheek and winked. "That remains to be seen, I think. All the more reason to get out of here as soon as politely possible."

She smiled at someone behind him, and he turned to see Lisa with two blue coffee mugs in hand. The heat felt wonderful in Mark's chilled hands, and she'd thoughtfully added enough cream and sugar to make the high-test brew palatable.

"Glad to see you on the surface again, Mark. Those guys are spinning quite the tale about you and Hackworth getting hit with a fire hose worth of water down there."

"They're probably not too far off from the truth. I had a second there when I thought…" He paused, surprised at a deep resurgence of fear, followed by an even harder rush of relief. He welcomed Beth's warm fingers twining through his own. "I'll just say I'm glad to be standing here."

"I'm glad of it too," Lisa said. "If you're feeling up to it tomorrow, we were wondering if you have time to meet with us. Me and McConvey, Hackworth and Grissom. See if we can get a start on keeping that water from building up again and get our folks back to work."

Mark nodded, trying to cast his mind out of his all-too-real visions of a pitch-black, watery grave and ahead to the next day.

"Yeah, I can do that. I mainly had paperwork and a few conference calls scheduled. This is more important for sure. We'll need some of the same folks I was planning to talk to involved anyway. Any time after eight is fine for me."

Lisa grinned and shook her head.

"Listen at you, after eight. I was thinking a lot more like ten would be a good time to start. That reminds me. Beth, I talked to Susan, and she's pushing your start time back to ten as well. Ready to call in help and extra scanners for things you can trust to someone else, to make up the time and keep you from being there half the night. High school kids who will get work-study credits. Just say the word and she'll get it done."

Beth blinked, and the slow smile Mark loved so much broke across her face.

"I'm saying the word, Lisa. Well, two words. *Thank you*."

She stepped forward and hugged Lisa, who Mark was stunned to see wiping her eyes when she stepped back.

"No need to thank me. I won't ever be able to thank you enough. None of us will. In fact, we're all going together and getting a pizza dinner with all the fixings delivered to your cabin in about an hour. I can tell you from experience that it reheats just fine if y'all have other things to do first. Both of you more than earned it."

She looked at Mark, winked, and said, "Nice ring." Then she strolled back over to the group of operators.

Mark had to glance down at the sparkling engagement ring on his pinky before he realized what she was talking about. He turned it back around to the inside.

"I'm getting the feeling I missed something. Probably more than one thing. Let me tell these guys good night and see what their plans are. Then maybe you can catch me up on the drive over to the cabin."

Beth slipped her arm around his waist, and he responded with one around her shoulders.

"Sounds great to me," she said. "Because as soon as we get there, I'll take off my necklace and you take off your lovely diamond ring. I appreciate all the help we got from the other side today. But I want you all to myself for the rest of the night even if we do have to wait long enough for that dinner delivery."

CHAPTER 20

BETH'S EXPECTATION of getting Mark alone and in private barely made it inside their cabin.

It was smaller and nicer than she expected, with every sign of recent construction designed to seem like it was a hundred years old.

Thick logs on the outside aged to look appropriately rustic, paired with an easy-care brown steel roof. An attached garage big enough to comfortably hold Mark's sedan took up almost half the entire building.

Inside, a tiny living room outfitted with comfortable furniture in outdoorsy browns and greens, paired with an efficient micro-kitchen full of granite and brushed stainless appliances. The floor's wooden planks probably were salvaged from honestly old buildings going by their rippled and knotty texture, and that gave an air of comforting authenticity to the whole place.

A double gas fireplace that passed through the living room wall into the bedroom didn't bother pretending to be rustic with sleek black fittings and glass doors.

What Beth and Mark were most interested in sat opposite a bedroom only big enough to hold a queen bed with space to walk around it, all dressed in the same cozy greens and browns and natural wood.

The bathroom was the only room that wasn't incredibly efficient in using every single inch and openly encouraging guests to spend their time in Isom Gap's spectacular settings outside. Pale gray slate tiles set off a charcoal gray tub that could fit three adults who didn't mind snuggling a bit. Or two who wanted to stretch out and relax for a long, much-needed soak.

Thankfully a separate shower tiled in the same slate as the floors waited off to the side to deal with the worst of the muck and grime Mark didn't shed when he stripped off his clothes in the garage. Beth had tried her best not to giggle at him streaking in his sock feet toward the front door, but she failed miserably.

About the time she kicked off her own boots to join him, Clina spoke up, and Beth heard Mark's Papaw saying pretty much the same thing a beat later.

"I'm real sorry to bother you again, Beth, and Mark too. But I get the feeling we might all need to listen to young Jacob for a minute."

Beth knew the ghostly intention of making sure Mark heard everything worked when he walked slowly back into the living room. He had a towel wrapped around his middle and he'd shed the filthy socks, but the dirt on his face showed he hadn't stepped into that shower yet.

He hadn't taken off his engagement ring, either.

"Is everything okay there?" Beth stepped forward and started up the gas fire, sending a pleasantly realistic flame dancing along the logs, along with a rush of warmth. "It sounds calmer."

For the first time in hours, she only heard typical background sounds of spectral conversation rather than arguing and shouting.

"Don't know for sure if it will ever be *calm* here," Papaw said. "But some of the worst of the bad feeling might of gone out of everyone. Like letting the infection out of a bad cut so it can try to heal up."

Mark shivered, and Beth saw goosebumps on his bare arms and legs.

"Can Jacob wait for a couple of minutes?" she said. "Mark is still half-frozen. Once he gets out of the shower and puts on a warm robe, we'll listen as long as Jacob wants to talk."

She didn't say it out loud, but she hoped Jacob wouldn't want to talk *all* that long.

She still had plans for Mark that didn't involve company, or either one of them being cold.

"I reckon Jacob can cool his heels for a bit longer," Clina said, a laugh clear in her voice. "Tell that feller to get cleaned up so you can keep him good and warm, Beth. Promise we won't keep you too long."

Mark grinned when Beth pointed toward the bathroom, then scurried back in and started the shower.

Beth shed her own jacket and rinsed her face in the bathroom sink, ignoring the very sensible urge to step into the glass-fronted shower now steamed up with hot water. Her next stop was the remarkably well-supplied kitchen, where she found hot cocoa mix, huge navy-blue mugs from the Isom Gap Historical Society, and an electric kettle. By the time Mark walked back out, wrapped in a white terrycloth robe and looking far more respectable, she was settled on the overstuffed sofa with her own sock feet on a huge footstool aimed toward the fire.

He had the good sense to grab a fuzzy blanket covered with brilliant autumn leaves from a chair on the way over.

Beth tried to smooth his damp, crazy-corkscrew hair while he tucked the blanket close around his legs and feet. Warm bundle created and tucked close against her, Mark grabbed her hands and laughed.

"There's not a chance of calming this ornery mess down after the day it's had. I'll get it wrangled before work tomorrow. I hope getting myself too neat and tidy tonight would turn out to be a waste of time."

Gazing into his bright green eyes, the reality of his near-miss threatened to drown Beth as thoroughly as he might have been under all those tons of rock. She pulled her hands free and kissed him hard and deep, holding his head so he couldn't move away until she had enough.

"You're right," she whispered against his lips when she finally let go. "I've still got plans for you and that bathtub. And that bed."

"The second we're finished up here," Mark breathed, "I'll race you right back in there."

A not at all subtle cough that didn't come from any living throat set both of them to giggling, and Beth knew she had the same caught-out-kid expression Mark did.

"Okay, we're respectable now," she said, picking up her mug and handing the other to Mark as he put his arm around her. "Respectable as we ever are, anyway."

She took a long drink of the hot cocoa, letting the dark chocolate with the perfect touch of spicy heat soothe her nerves. After a good drink of his own, Mark leaned toward her and whispered "Thank you." They both put the mugs on a coffee table covered with a tablecloth with apples embroidered all over it.

"I reckon that will just have to do," Clina said. "You took long enough you'll have to listen to more than one talking now. Can't do much about that."

Beth settled her head on Mark's shoulder and one hand on his thigh, on the soft robe rather than his skin. For now.

"We're ready. Are you still there, Jacob?"

Her impatience softened at the hesitant and obviously youthful sound of his voice.

"I'm right here, ma'am, and I sure do appreciate you both for taking the time. I reckon it's time to set things straight about what happened to me now that I finally got the chance."

He took a deep, shaky breath loud enough to hear.

"Everything's going to be okay, Jacob," Mark said, resting his cheek against Beth's hair. "It could be that what you did trying to get through to me was the only way things could get better on both sides."

"I sure do thank you for saying so. That might make what I got to say a little easier to get out. Truth is what happened to me was my doing, least part of it was. My own damn fault for playing a stupid game instead of paying mind to my work. See, I got into a wager with two other boys working at the same mill as me. Same two I chased down before, that's staring at me right now."

He paused, and Beth heard a low murmur of voices talking in the background. Soothing voices. After a second, Jacob went on. Beth imagined his pale, thin face set loose from imprisonment in the old photograph, his fine hair moving in the breeze.

"We was all trying to see who could stack up that cut lumber the highest. Can't remember who come up with that dumb idea, but it turned out the same no matter what."

Beth spoke into the silence, her heart aching at the thought of such young boys working in such a dangerous job, where silly teenager mistakes could so easily mean life or death.

"Carlis Grissom and Eural Joe McConvey, wasn't it?"

"Yes ma'am, that's just who it was. I'm sorry to say I made good on my boast that I could beat 'em both. A couple days after the whole crew broke the record for putting out the most cut boards had ever been done in these mountains. I'm even deeper ashamed to admit what got me killed was climbing up on top of that great stack of lumber, whooping and hollering like a pure fool."

Beth shuddered, thinking of the towering stacks in Deborah Fleming's photo. She didn't want to imagine heavy wood piled even higher, much less a slender boy on top of it all.

"We all do things when we're young boys," Mark's Papaw said, his voice gentle. "Things grown men seem to forget all about when they see boys acting the very same way. I hate no one who remembered was there to stop you. I would have done my very best."

"Oh no, it wasn't that way with no one trying," Jacob protested. "See, that's what makes this whole thing the worst of all. One of the men did try to stop me, then tried to catch me when the whole pile came tumbling down. Mr. Hackworth here did everything he could, all the way to getting himself hurt. No, every last bit of it was me taking leave of all my good sense, and more people than I could ever know suffered for it all these years."

A new voice spoke up then, obviously the much deeper, rougher tones of a grown man. The broad-shouldered, bearded man from the photo had entered the scene.

"You need to listen to me, Jacob, and pay heed to what I'm telling you. Mr. Hersch here was speaking the truth about the empty-headed things we all get up to when we're half-grown. Girls do much the same, but it seems to me they don't get themselves hurt near as often. I had an idea what you and the other two cooked up between you. I didn't do near enough to stop it, and that's my own shame to carry."

Mark shifted, and Beth moved enough to see his face.

"I'm guessing you're Mr. Hackworth?" he said. "Purvis Hackworth? I'm Mark Hersch, proud grandson of the man standing there with you. I'd sure like to ask you a couple of questions if you don't mind."

"I am Purvis Lee Hackworth, and since I never have been asked a question by a living man since I passed over, I'd be happy to answer best I can."

Mark raised his eyebrows, looking as close to nervous as Beth had ever seen him.

"I don't mean to call attention away from what Jacob is trying to say," he said, "or you, or anyone else there. I'll just take up a minute or two. I do want to thank all of you. Strange as it might sound, what you did there tonight might have saved a lot of lives here. If that water had gotten a whole lot worse, it might have broken loose with a full crew under the ground."

A general sound of wonderment—all gasps and sighs and a bit of amazed laughter—rose up from across the veil. Mark grinned when his Papaw spoke up.

"Hear that, Jacob? And you, Purvis Lee? I'm speaking to Carlis and Eural Joe, too. That's a real good thing you all did, going a long way toward making a wrong thing right. Go ahead, water bug."

"Thank you, mud bug. What I want to ask you, Mr. Hackworth, is how did you find your way back here? To Isom Gap? I heard you moved away a while before you passed."

Beth was confused for a second, then she noticed Mark rubbing his thumb over the ring on his finger, the movement making the diamonds catch the firelight.

He was really asking about his grandmother. About why she'd never shown up back in Bountyfield where she was buried so many years later.

She reached for his hand and held it to her lips, then clasped it in both of hers.

"Don't know how much I can help you," Purvis said, "but I'll sure do my best. Enough time has passed over on this side that I can't manage to carry that grudge I held for so long. Some folks hold onto theirs for eternity, I guess, but I'm just not made that way. I know the three of you was just boys then with no idea what your words and actions could do. Some of those words sent me a long way off from Isom Gap and I never did plan to come back."

"I sure do hope it wasn't me that made you run off," Jacob said in a quiet voice.

Purvis laughed, and it couldn't have been more different from Chip Hackworth's loud guffaw. This was deeper and more than a little bit sad.

"Not gonna go down that road, not with any of you boys. I may not look like it, not like I did when I passed away or when I was living back in Hidden Springs. Those years fell away when I found my way back here. But I lived a long, long time. Maybe *because* that terrible limp I picked up trying to save Jacob kept me out of dangerous work like at the mill or in a coal mine. Kept me from getting tore up again. Anyway, other thing I learned is folks get a chance to learn from their mistakes if they live long enough."

A new voice spoke then, a boy Jacob's age Beth didn't recognize.

"Once in a great while folks can figure it out even if they don't live to see gray hair on their faces. You might not remember me after so much time. I'm Carlis Grissom. And I'm real sorry, Mr. Hackworth. I never should have told all them rumors about you being the one that caused Jacob to get killed. Me and Eural Joe, I guess we got scared the blame would fall on us. Probably should have, too."

The sound of shuffling feet and the rising and falling hiss

of whispers rose up—not that much different from a restless crowd made up of the living. Clina interrupted the fidgety noise with her usual sharp words.

"Reckon you're gonna speak up, Eural Joe? Or stand there shifting from one foot to the other? Seems to me something worth fighting over with these other boys is worth saying out loud."

"I'm real sorry too, Mr. Hackworth. Like Carlis said, we should have took all the blame for what happened to Jacob. Not tried to stir up trouble and keep everyone worked up and angry at one another. The bad stories we told about you was even worse, Jacob. We all had that dumb idea about the contest together. Wasn't right of us to make it out to be all your fault."

Beth moved so she could whisper close to Mark's ear, as if that would keep Clina from hearing.

"Sounds like the bad blood is draining away with the water and the dead spot. But no one answered your question."

He kissed her cheek and shook his head.

"There may not be an answer, not for this. Papaw says sometimes people never show up at all."

They both froze when Purvis Lee Hackworth raised his voice loud enough to sound like he was right there in the compact living room with them.

"I can't say there's no answer at all, Mr. Hersch. It's just that none of the ones I know of are easy."

CHAPTER 21

Mark's heart seemed to swell within his body, pushing out a flood of hope and fear and excitement that threatened to overwhelm him.

He'd never been quite as close to his Granny as his Papaw, but he missed her terribly all the same. And so much talking to his Papaw constantly brought home how awful it was for him.

All these years in the next life without the love of his first one by his side.

So deep down he did everything he could to ignore it, Mark was also afraid of what might happen when his and Beth's time came to cross over. Turned out knowing the answer to one of humanity's greatest questions stirred up more trouble than it settled.

Would they never be able to find each other again no matter how badly they wanted to?

He squeezed her close against him, grateful for her warmth even though the chill from his experience with a miniature flood had almost left him between her body and the wonderful hot chocolate and the fire.

The heat she provided went a hell of a lot deeper than his mere skin and bones.

"What do you mean by that, Mr. Hackworth?" he said. "What answers do you know, easy or hard?"

"Well, I only know how it's been for me. Might be different for everyone else in the world. But what drew me back here after a lifetime and years of my deathtime away seems tied up to that dead spot in the world. All I knew was something pulling at me, tugging day and night so I couldn't rest or think on anything else. Got to where I was tore up so bad that I wasn't acting like myself. Got it into my head to leave Hidden Springs and just lit out walking."

"How long did it take?" Beth said. "Can you tell?"

"Wish I could help you there, but I couldn't say. About the best we can do with time is knowing when someone else passes and finding out how long since we did that way. I don't know how to mark the years or any people in Isom Gap after so much time slipped by. I sure am sorry."

Mark closed his eyes, wishing he could give his Papaw a hug. Beth's arms going around him helped considerably.

"That's okay, you helped plenty," he said. "As far as what we *can* figure out, I'm hoping we can get the weakness on our side of the world repaired and keep that water from building up. I hope it works the same for you with that dead spot. Maybe you'll be able to get yourself back to Hidden Springs, if you want to."

Mr. Hackworth chuckled, and Mark couldn't keep himself from smiling.

"Far as I can tell, I'll be here as long as they need me. Long as someone remembers who I am, that might be part of it. I hope whoever you're searching for finds the way real soon. Listen, I hate for you to think I'm being rude and running off, but I got more talking to do with these three young men. Make sure all of us are running clear instead of getting all gunked up like before. I do thank you all for what you helped us do. Maybe we can all talk again real soon."

Mark and Beth added their thanks to Papaw and Clina, then listened as three young voices and one older one moved away.

"I wouldn't jump right to feeling like all hope is gone," Clina said, speaking softer than usual. "All this talking across the veil business is new for folks on both sides, and it took me many a long year to get through no matter how you measure. If I'm understanding you right, Mark, you holding on to something dear to your family is what lets you hear us, especially your papaw."

Mark held his right hand up, turning it so the diamonds caught the mellow light of the fire.

"That's right, Clina. This is my grandmother's engagement ring, or it was. I guess it still is, but I hope Beth will keep it once I find something else to wear or carry with me." He laughed under his breath and winked at Beth. "For a while at least. Whether she wants me to or not, I want to find her a ring all her own."

"Then I sure would say you never know what might come to pass," Clina said. "Sounds to me like folks both living and dead have an attachment to that ring. And it makes your tie to your papaw that much stronger. I ain't never been the kind to make a promise I can't keep, but could be it will draw your granny home to Bountyfield the same way the dead spot drew Purvis Lee Hackworth back home to Isom Gap."

Mark closed his eyes and held his face against Beth's hair, breathing in her scent.

"I hope that's true. I'm pleased as I can be to have more of a connection no matter what else happens. Lisa's sister took a while to find her way there, so it's not impossible. You think you'll be able to help Lisa find something that will work to talk to her sister?"

"I think so," Beth said. "Lisa said she has something in mind, and I'm sure you do for your Papaw. What I keep coming back to is what got all of this stirred up in the first place. The rip in the veil in Estonoa that let the moths through seemed to start with the work on the dam at the lake. Nothing like that happened here, right?"

Mark sat back and retrieved his cocoa, handing the other one to Beth. It had cooled considerably but still tasted wonderful.

"Not that I know of. But there was one big change that I think Purvis Lee Hackworth would understand. Our Chip Hackworth only came back here a couple of years ago and got involved in the mine, right near that weak spot. My guess is that got the other side stirred up kind of like it did here. Does that sound right to you, Papaw, from what you've seen and heard?"

"There's a real funny thing in this place that don't match up with the way things work in Bountyfield. Seems to me like the line between us is...thinner, maybe, and not just at that dead place. Or easier to pass through, like cutting through butter instead of trying to bust through ice. Folks affect each other more in both directions. So what you're saying makes sense to me, water bug. I know you and Beth are wore out and want some time to yourselves. But I got one other thing to tell you that might help you rest easy tonight."

The faint sound of a car door slamming outside could only mean their pizza dinner had arrived. Beth squeezed Mark's knee as she got to her feet.

"Stay right where you are. I don't want you flashing the driver after you streaked in here from the garage."

"That's probably for the best," he said with a smile. "I could use an easy rest tonight, Papaw. What is it?"

"Know how that dead spot was shrinking itself right down to nothing? Now I see the faintest blush of green around the edges. Might not get too far with winter coming on, but it's there. I'd wager the ground will sprout right up in the spring better than it has in years. You said it true about the folks here doing a real good thing. You and Beth did too, hear me water bug?"

Mark waved at the young woman making the delivery, then watched Beth line up a surprising number of boxes on the kitchen counter and dainty kitchen table. She didn't make a move to open any of them, apparently remembering Lisa's advice that it all reheated well as much as he did.

"I hear you loud and clear, mud bug. Right back at you and Clina. I hope that means folks on this side will get along a bit better, too. We'll talk in the morning, okay? Love you."

"Love you right back."

Mark stood and stretched, then folded his blanket and left it on the sofa. He didn't take the ring off, but the sounds of the ghost world faded down to a low background noise.

Maybe his Papaw could turn the connection up and down, or maybe they'd all moved away somehow. He'd have to ask Beth if Clina did the same.

Later.

Maybe when they finally made it back out here for what promised to be a very late-night feast.

She met him in the middle of the room in a long, deep, chocolate-scented kiss that chased away every last bit of the day's stress and fear and worry.

"Ready for that bath now?" she said, taking his hand and a step toward the bathroom that he was all too glad to follow. "I think we've earned a bit of privacy."

"I'm always ready for anything with you, private or not. Lead the way."

ABOUT KARI

The daughter, granddaughter, and great-granddaughter of coal miners, Kari Kilgore's wanderlust and imagination lead her all over the world on grand adventures. Her heart and family bring her home to her native Appalachian Mountains of Virginia. From that solid base and with the help of the ever-changing lens of her imagination, she brings those adventures to life in fiction.

She's never met ghosts or haints in caves or the occasional coal mine in real life. But she never doubts it could happen.

Kari writes fantasy, science fiction, romance, mystery, and contemporary fiction, and she's happiest when she surprises herself. She lives with her husband Jason A. Adams, various house critters, and wildlife they're better off not knowing more about.

The Confidential Adventure Club

For Kari's exclusive free After The End stories and deleted scenes, discounts, early pre-sale releases, adorable pet photos, and a whole lot more not available anywhere else, join us in The Club.

Hope to see you there!

www.KariKilgore.com
www.SpiralPublishing.net
www.ConfidentialAdventureClub.com

ALSO BY KARI KILGORE

I hope you enjoyed reading *Sorrows in the Earth* as much as I enjoyed writing it. For more with Beth, Mark, Clina, and Walt, don't miss *Songs in the Mountain*, *Secrets in the Land*, and more from the *Voices Through Time Series*.

For more adventures from the Appalachian Mountains of Virginia and around the region, and in many genres, head over to www.KariKilgore.com/TalesFromAppalachia.

If you're in a romantic mood, visit www.KariKilgore.com/Romance. For more fantasy of many kinds, visit www.KariKilgore.com/Fantasy.

Be the first to know about release dates and check out more of my fiction, including almost every genre, at www.KariKilgore.com.

The Voices through Time Series:

Songs in the Mountain

Secrets in the Land

Sorrows in the Earth

Walking the Ghosts: A Voices through Time Novella

The Storms of Future Past Series:

Dreaming the Storm

Joining the Storm

Into the Storm

Fighting the Storm

Storms of the Heart: A Storms of Future Past Romance

Storms of Future Past Books One through Four Collection

The Odd Society:

Independent by Means of Magic

Protected by Means of Magic

Dispatches from the Galaxy Stories:

Restricted Species

The Becalmed

The Garbage Belt

Plurapod Pathogen

The Changes Cascade

Novels:

Until Death

The Dream Thief

Hand Me Downs

Protecting Her Own

The Coffee Bomb and the Corporate Spy

The Great Gold Record Heist

Novellas:

Legacy of the Land

In the Pines

DNA Never Lies

The Box of Possibilities

Murder at the Fabulous Feline Emporium

Collections:

Fantastic Women: A Dark Fantasy Novella Trio

Fantastic Shorts: Volume 1

Near Future Forward (with Jason A. Adams)

Fantastic Shorts: Volume 2

Partners in Romance (with Jason A. Adams)

Dispatches from the Galaxy: A Space Opera Novella Trio

Fantastic Shorts: Volume 3

Escape into Romance: A Collection of Sweet Beginnings

Stepping Out of Reality: Short Spells of Appalachian Magic

Facing Down Extraordinary: A Series of Ordinary Heroes

Hacking Cybercrime: Dana Sanderson Short Mysteries

Shadows Mountain Deep (with Jason A. Adams)

Investigations Beyond Belief: The Initial Adventures of Deb Powers: Otherworldly PI

Passages in the Real World: Six Stories of Life's Transitions

Fantastic Side Trips: Side Characters Take Center Stage

A Kaleidoscope of Cat Tales: Five Stories of Cats and People Who Love Them

A Tapestry of Holiday Tales: Winter Adventures from the Odds and Endings Bookstore

Uncommon Holidays: A Different Side of the Season (with Jason A. Adams)

Aunties Among Us: Five Tales of Fabulous Women

Four-Legged Heroes: When Pets Rescue People

Partnership in Crime: Six Journeys to Justice